KNOW YOUR LOCAL

Buckman Publishing LLC
est. 2018
1448 NE 28th Ave
Portland, Oregon 97232
buckmanjournal.com

Congratulations! A Buckman production is in your hands! We're an unorthodox operation that continues the daredevil tradition of literature, printing new sparks that ignite imagination. Proudly independent, Buckman's defiant attitude aims to inspire and increase readership in greater society.

Buckman operates from our home in the upper left of Turtle Island at the confluence of the Whilamut and Wimahl rivers, among the waters and lands of the Cayuse, Clackamas, Multnomah, St'pulmsh (Cowlitz) Umatilla, Walla Walla, and Watlala peoples.

ALL RIGHTS RESERVED

Words © 2025 Benjamin Kessler
Cover & Artwork © 2025 Forest Wolf Kell
Book Design: Ellen Robinette
Typefaces: Garamond Premier Pro, SARABUN,
FRANKLIN GOTHIC ATF

ISBN: 9798990017467   LCCN: 2024949865

No part of this publication may be reproduced or transmitted in any form—electronic, mechanical, photocopying, recording, or otherwise—without prior written permission of the publisher.

This is a work of fiction. Names, characters, places, and incidents either are the products of the author's imagination or are used fictitiously. Any resemblance to actual persons, living or dead, businesses, companies, events, or locales is entirely coincidental.

READ THIS BOOK WHEREVER BOOKS CAN BE READ

THE PINNACLE

A NOVELLA BY BENJAMIN KESSLER

ARTWORK BY FOREST WOLF KELL

FOR L + K

I was pushing coin at Canteen when the call came.

"You can be ready how soon?" The voice belonged to Noor, my boss. I could tell she was agitated by the edge in her voice.

"Hello to you, too." I rocked into the cabinet with my hips and a *No Tilting :(:(:(* message flashed on the scuffed marquee.

"Yes, yes, how soon then?"

"Not until Sunday. I'm off this week." A few quarters rattled down into the return tray. I celebrated by polishing off the last of what was then my third beer before placing the empty in line with its comrades atop the machine's display.

"Not anymore. Be ready at 1700."

"Oh no, I'm not—"

She hung up before I could protest further.

I placed my phone facedown on top of the console and looked up at the Zephyr Lite clock hanging above the bar. I had three hours. I rubbed the tired from my eyes; my fingers reeked of change, metal-stink like blood.

"Sounds like you won't be staying long." Hermann Hilton appeared by my side and slid a coin into the slot. He smelled as though he'd come straight from his shift at the polystyrene recycling center. "Mind if I cut in?"

"Fuck off stain, that's my stack. I've been working on it all afternoon." I took my phone and tucked it into the waistband of my jeans.

"Well you better hope it falls in the next thirty seconds." He dragged his fingers across the glass, leaving oily streaks. "From what I gather you just got your peach picked, and ain't no way you're making it to the city in less than a few hours."

He was right: if I wanted to get home and pack with any time to catch the Manhattan Express Megabus I'd need to leave now.

"Fine. But no one can make love to this machine like I can, and she knows it." I gestured for the bartender to put a longneck Fratler's in a paper bag and then pulled a quarter from the return, which I placed in the front pouch of Hermann's coveralls. "Next play's on me."

I gave Hermann the finger and retrieved my road beer before pushing through the swinging door and into the afternoon sun. I'd left my meager winnings in the bar, two-hour's work totaling less than five dollars. The kinds of coin pushers I played, those that paid out in real money rather than redemption tickets, had been made illegal in Connecticut a few years back, part of a larger crackdown on gambling nationwide. I didn't have a gambling problem, but I did worry for the day I would show up at Canteen and find the machine repossessed by the Department of Consumer Protection. I've never responded well to dispossession.

As I began the walk back to the house, I thought I heard the machine back inside clattering, signaling the win I'd been working toward. Though I couldn't be sure it wasn't just cube ice falling into a glass.

I took the steep way back, past the abandoned high school and shuttered Department of Motor Vehicles and the minimart that sold individual cigarettes, hoping to sweat out a bit of the alcohol and appear less buzzed when I got home, a tactic I'd convinced myself worked and didn't just leave me winded and rank. At the top of the hill, I stopped to catch my breath and looked out over the Sound, toward the faraway outline of the Long Island shore I so envied as a child. Many of New Haven's beaches—of which there were few—had been privatized when I was young, the result of a massive budget shortfall the city council had, for decades, failed to address. My father, frugal to a fault, couldn't be asked to spend the two-hundred dollars on the pass that granted access to the newly exclusive coastline, so we spent any seaside time the only way we could: huddled with everyone else at The Point where rocks tore holes in our swim trunks and algae thick as snot made swimming impossible.

I began the descent toward the house, my shins bearing the juddering brunt of an unsteady body. I knew home was close by the harsh braying of donkeys, a drove of which were stabled at the lot three down from our own. The owner, a thin Dutch bachelor, wore coveralls two sizes larger than he needed, giving him a clownish appearance. We'd never exchanged even a passing friendliness, something mirrored in his animals, which stood impassively at the fence as I walked by. I envied the Dutchman's acreage, if not the shit he had to shovel from it.

My relationship with the Dutchman typified the relationships I had with most of my neighbors, a sort of tacit indifference toward one another. Perhaps this was because of the high turnover in rental properties or the gradual erosion of socialization in the modern Internet doldrums. Embry and I owned our house—though it's more accurate to say that whichever bank currently possessed the rights to my mortgage were the true owners; it seemed we got a letter once every six months or so informing us of its ceaseless motion—so we were rooted, at least for the time being.

When I got home, but before I went inside, I stashed

the unopened beer in a length of coiled garden hose so that I could covertly recover it on my way out.

"She knows you're not on again until Sunday, right? It's right there in the contract that you get a full seven days."

I caught Embry during a session. Between print lay-out gigs she painted traditional portraits for those who still wanted them, maybe one or two appointments a month. The money wasn't exceptional, but it gave her an opportunity to, in her words, escape her lizard brain for three or four hours.

I apologized to the pink-faced young man—who I would later learn was the junior vice president at a bank—that sat patiently in our living room, hands crossed in manufactured dignity, as I made all kinds of noise rooting around for my things. Would Embry paint in the prodigious sweat that accumulated at the gentlemen's brow and in the folds of his neck?

"Don't look down, it casts shadows," she said to the man, miming a double chin with her hands. She stepped away from the canvas and brandished the tip of her paintbrush at me. "I don't see why they can't just wait it out. It's only four days." At the word "four" she stabbed the brush forward and coral droplets dotted the plastic sheet beneath her feet.

"I know, but what can I do?"

"I can think of a few things," she muttered, turning back to the portrait.

After pawing through a hamper in the laundry room, I'd found one boot cover but not the other and closed my eyes hard as though to will its location into my mind. The booze in my blood scattered my thoughts, and trying to retrace my steps became like attempting to rest my hand on a hot burner.

"No, Tom, like this." Embry walked over and placed one paint-smeared hand on each of the bank man's temples, pointing him the way she wanted. "Now don't go limp on me." She returned to her easel and began to mix oils. "The way I see it they should at least give you back the days off at some point."

I could only just hear her, partially because she had the handle of a paintbrush in her mouth but mainly because I was digging through the hall closet for my high-visibility vest.

I'd resisted drinking the beer on the walk home. I didn't want my breath to smell especially of alcohol, but rather the odor of exertion, a musk which I attempted to heighten by jogging in place around the corner from the house, in full view of the impassive donkeys. If she could sense the veil of cigarette smoke and sugary liquor that cloaked me while in the bar, she didn't immediately let on, perhaps to not start a fight in front of the clammy man in our living room. To explain my absence, I'd told Embry that I was going to the hardware store to buy wood screws, an hour's walk each way from our condo. Walking to and from various errands had become an easy way to hide my excursions to Canteen. What would I say when she asked where the screws I had supposedly bought were? Lie, tell her stock was low these days, that the price had gone up, but wasn't it good that I gave it a try? Lying came easy, a muscle toned by years of covering my own tracks.

Even if she did discover where I'd actually been, I was still doing better than a few months ago, when simply rousing me from bed took a crane and my pillowcase was consistently stained with vomit. I'd trimmed my visits to the bar by half, only going twice a week and never on days when I had obligations. Wasn't that progress?

I told Embry that I wasn't sure about making up the time lost from the extra work and pulled my vest from beneath a stack of folded towels. I then threw it onto a pile of work clothes growing beside the front door.

"Well, you should ask."

I ventured upstairs to fill my toiletry bag and in the process of carrying it to the bathroom a pocket-sized bottle of Irish whiskey fell from it and onto the carpet. Emergency liquor bought in Manhattan after my last shift. I retrieved the bottle and stowed it between the mattress and box spring. Would Embry change the sheets? I moved it to my bedside drawer, stashed behind a tangle of charging cables.

After stuffing socks and underwear into my duffle, I fell onto the bedspread and stretched out across the mattress. I knew this was a bad idea; I could so easily fall asleep. Not from the day drinking—three beers was light work—but because I'd been up late the night before assembling shelves in the basement. My father, himself a recovering alcoholic—*always in recovery*, he would tell me, *never recovered*—preached absorption. "You can't drink a beer," he said, "if you have a power tool in each hand." Was I an alcoholic? The doctor's checklist said so. Embry insisted so. So I'd taken to building things, project after project, a joint penance and distraction.

We're going to have a whole new house by February, I overheard Embry say on the phone to her mother. Kitchen cabinets were next on my list, then a bathroom remodel. One time I actually was at the hardware store there had been a branded cooler on sale, and the only thing I could think of was how good a beer would taste pulled from it and sweating in my begrimed hand.

But Embry had banned beer from the house. And gin. And wine. And cigarettes because she knew that nothing accompanied one better than other forms of other poisons. So it was just me, and my thoughts, and a new screw gun and laser level and bandsaw. At home, anyway.

I stopped my eyes from closing by pinching the inside of my thigh then sat up and checked Zone, the social media app made specifically for the employees of Robison-Moon, the construction company through which

I was under contract as a journeyman electrician. Zone most certainly mined our data for unknown purposes—it requested access to our cameras, microphone, photos, and even calculator—but using it came with a five percent reduction on our annual healthcare premium, so most everyone signed up.

I messaged Saeed, one of my coworkers, knowing he'd be using the app. He was almost always on Zone, commenting on the posts of our peers and uploading photos of the anime trading card game he collected, which he had tried and failed to teach me on multiple occasions. When, after our shifts were over and our phones had been returned to us, he would spend most of the evening hunched over Zone, stopping only to pick at cold chana masala, one of the dinnertime options Robison-Moon afforded its predominantly South Asian workforce.

I messaged him, asking if he knew what was going on and he responded immediately that he'd heard someone had gotten hurt, that the team had been given time off, but that he wasn't sure. Zone couldn't confirm anything.

Maybe they walked out, I suggested. Saeed said he didn't think so, but the idea wasn't so implausible. Conditions under Robison-Moon never approached abuse, but it was far from desk work, and tradies of all varieties had unceremoniously exited jobsites over less. While I was no apologist for how we were treated—long, isolated hours and nights spent in windowless, fart-filled barracks—the money was enough that Embry could work part-time, though not so much that we could afford to live far from where we'd grown up. It's possible that I had passed the house I currently live in at some point during my childhood, riding my bike between laundromats so I could look for stray coins beneath the machines.

RIP to our weekend plans, I typed.
How's Embry taking it?
Poorly.

Embry had never professed to being a fan of the work I did. The schedule—one week on, one week off—gave her ample time to herself, but was accompanied by a loneliness I'd only discovered after seeing a friend-finder app open on her phone, an avenue to companionship she had at one time publicly mocked. Even if she traveled to New York during my workweek there'd be no way to see one another, as no one but contracted workers were allowed at the jobsite. Robison-Moon included several videos in our onboarding about how to spot emotional changes in life partners as a result of the stressful schedule, PSAs generated as the result of a public lawsuit. *Watch for the warning signs*, the AI-generated voice urged us. *Weight gain or loss, difficulty sleeping, sudden changes in mood, indicators of substance abuse such as empty bottles or secretive behavior.* I hadn't seen any of these. Surely, I would have noticed. How could anyone keep something like that a secret?

Most of my coworkers either lived alone or had left partners overseas in their home countries. Aside from my boss, the entirety of my team was male, which meant that Noor slept in the women's barracks alone, a monastic life that no one else knew anything about. Did she sleep on a different bed each night? Did she walk around naked? Her barracks were an entire floor below our own, bottled away by an elevator access code. The other men were tempted to treat her differently on the jobsite, more delicately, perhaps, but she was just as crass and hard-nosed as any of them. Whether this was merely an adaptation to the setting or her actual personality I wasn't sure. At times the jobsite and barracks felt like a frat house, just without the prospect of anything fun happening, and, of course, no booze.

I told Saeed I would meet him at the jobsite and took one last moment to savor the comfort of my bed. I buried my face in Embry's pillow in an attempt to capture her smell, the scent of her lilac shampoo lingering on the slipcase. God, it was only Wednesday.

I shoved the rest of my clothes into the bag and went back downstairs where I found Linda, our salt-and-pepper cairn terrier, near the front door, her body curled to fit the shape of my hard hat as she dozed in a sunbeam. I watched as Embry blended tones on the bank man's tie, swirling the hues together. She shifted her weight from one foot to the other, then back, then again. She ran a hand across the front of her sweatpants, leaving a line of paint through a bleach spot. I picked up my hard hat, which Linda protested by nipping at my fingers, and walked to Embry's side, whispering to her that I was leaving. In response, she tapped her cheek twice. I gave the indicated spot a delicate peck, causing the bank man to look away sheepishly, as though he were seeing something he shouldn't. On noticing this, I kissed Embry hard on the mouth and lingered. I turned to leave but she grabbed hold of my arm. Her face and eyes moved as though she were in deep thought, like she was attempting to untangle some knot in her mind. She made me promise I'd call her later.

I told her I would, of course I would, and she let me go, wiping our kiss from her lips.

Back outside I checked that I was out of sight before retrieving the beer from the hose, waving away a few flies that had landed on the lid which I twisted off, muffling the sound with my palm. It was a ten-minute trip to the bus station and I walked as slowly as possible to savor the taste, knowing that it would be the last for over a week.

We'd relocated to this part of New Haven—now nicknamed "The Stink Side" due to its steady accumulation of chemical processing facilities serviced by the port—specifically because of its proximity to the bus terminal, even though our little condo now reeked of diesel from the asphalt plant. It was just one of the many concessions Embry had made after we'd moved in together. She could no longer easily visit her parents or sister or friends up in Hartford, and she'd lost many freelance clients in the transition; both of which had nested in me an unassailable guilt. The fact of the matter was that I made more money, enough that Embry could work when she pleased, and we could eat out at the Silver Sawback on a whim. Plus, I'd grown up only ten blocks from where we now lived, my parents still in the same craftsman house with the peeling green paint and the garage door that sagged in its tracks like a busted mouth.

I walked by an overgrown trio of baseball diamonds, the legion gophers squeaking at one another across the infield. The vehicles that passed on the frontage road were still gas-powered, coughing and spurting in their death throes, unlike the electric four-doors that prowled silently through the city center, their owners playing smartphone Scrabble with the car in autopilot. This made the bridge over the Quinnipiac—the river that bisected the city—particularly brackish as castes that naturally drew themselves became evident. West of the river, near the University and the new development which surrounded it, the air seemed sweeter, the streets cleaner, the graffiti having been reclaimed as "street art" by academics and investment bankers. On The Stink Side, mornings were filled with the smell of garbage being turned over at the landfills that abutted the river or the juddering of planes landing at the less modern of the city's two airports. At The Stink Side's infrequent bus stops, bench ads hawked services for personal injury lawyers and skincare specialists who could take fat from your ass and inject it into your lips, two types of visual vomit that petered out as you crossed the river. As a frequent bus rider, I was an expert in these ads, their toll-free numbers scribed into my brain. Embry and I didn't have a car anymore. We jointly decided it wasn't worth it after the gas tax got raised for the fifth year in a row. "One less mouth to feed," she joked as we walked from the bus exchange near the shuttered adult day care, six bags of groceries split between us.

Once at the bus terminal, I flashed my Robison-Moon badge as proof of fare to an otherwise disinterested driver.

"You can't bring that on," they said as I swung my bag up onto the overhead rack.

"Excuse me?"

"Either drain it or pitch it, but no open container on the vehicle."

I'd nearly forgotten about the bottle in my hand, its shape like an extension of my arm. I finished what little remained, mostly backwash lukewarm from the heat of my palm, and ran to toss the empty into a trash can before jumping back into the bus. You could never find a recycling bin on The Stink Side.

I settled into a seat near the front and fashioned my jacket into a makeshift pillow. I was nursing a pleasant buzz, enough that I hoped I might fall asleep somewhere before Bridgeport. As the bus shook to life, I noticed the driver monologuing into a hands-free headset, something about a dog with fleas forced to sleep in the garage.

The bus was combustion, one of only a few still running, and as it shuddered out of the parking bay my drowsiness became amplified by the sun tilting just so through the window. I popped on headphones strictly for the quiet and closed my eyes.

I'd ridden a bus similar to this nearly every day back in college, sputtering away from my dorm at Southern Connecticut State to the municipal airfield where I worked weekends as a mechanic's apprentice. That was ten years ago, when things were only just starting to turn over to renewables, and a tinge of shame would materialize in my stomach as I passed by the Yale campus with its fleet of electric trams and roofs covered by photovoltaic arrays.

"Southern's a fine enough school," my father would say, poring over pages of schematics for whatever contraption he was obsessed with at the moment. He was no engineer, had never gone to college—*it would have been a waste,* he had told me once, though whether he meant it would have been a waste *on him* or *because of him* remained unclear—and instead made a living installing drywall. But he had his hobbies, chief of which was an insatiable tinkering. He'd see some gadget online, say, a knife blade polisher, and try to improve it, reinvent it somehow.

"What if it could sharpen at the same time? Or even scale a fish?" he'd ask over dinner, gesturing at the rest of us with his fork. "You'd never need another knife the rest of your life." The very next day he'd have rush-ordered the thing and disassembled it, plastic bits strewn across the salvaged drop-leaf table in the basement that constituted his workbench. I was allowed entrance into this space on the conditions that I wouldn't touch anything—everything, it seemed, was fragile and irreplaceable—and that I hand him whatever type of secondhand screwdriver he required, very few of which were used for anything but prying things apart which were meant to remain together. Occasionally teachable moments would arise, though I was no student and he no expert.

"You see this?" he would say, pointing with a bandaged finger, "this here is important to the whole apparatus. Paramount. Now if I could just figure out what it does…"

More often than not, these endeavors resulted in cardboard boxes full of busted components, stacks of which rose up toward the squat basement ceiling. My mother urged him to throw away the failures—though he would never call them this; rather, they were "experiments"—but his response was always the same: that he might need that stuff one day. "You never do know, after all," he would tell her. My older brother, while assembling a skateboard at the workbench, reminded me that all of it would one day be allocated between the two of us, the closest thing to any kind of inheritance.

On the rare chance his reinventions worked as planned, the end product got used only a few times before being pushed into some cobwebbed corner. I recall an electric bicycle picked up cheap at a yard sale that he modified to emit colorful sparks from the back wheel when pedaled.

"Is it safe?" my mother shouted at him as he navigated a wide, sparkly circle around our darkened cul-de-sac.

"What?" The rig that created the bright shower clicked and hummed loudly—some assemblage of bent sheet metal and chain. A crowd amassed, other families who knew my father only as the kind, odd gentlemen who punched tickets at high school football games. This was perhaps the first time he had displayed one of his creations. The Chaudharys waved at my mother from across the street and in response she buried her face in her robe.

"You're going to catch yourself on fire, Brian!" She pulled my brother and me close, as if to keep us from running into the street to meet certain immolation.

"I can't hear you," he yelled back. Through the particle rainbow that trailed behind him I could just make out the sincere and childlike smile spread across his face. He made us take pictures of him standing beside it, which he printed out and tacked up above his workbench, a reminder of success. He asked anyone else if they wanted to give it a try and was politely turned down by all. Of course, we never used the bike again after that. I think my mother eventually deposited it in the dumpster behind the Reddy Getter.

I drifted off not long after the bus merged onto I-95, sunlight baking my face and by the time a fire truck siren woke me up we were exiting the Lincoln Tunnel and the high-rises of Midtown sprang up around us. During my sleep an older gentleman with a constellation of acne took the seat beside mine. I watched him continually run a hand through his mustache as a court show with celebrity judges played on his tablet. I was happy to have slept through the tunnel. Navigating it felt like being in a coffin inside a coffin.

From the Port Authority Bus Terminal it was only a six block walk to the jobsite, which sat in the space that formerly housed Madison Square Garden and Penn Station. When the city moved the largely defunded train station (had I ever ridden a passenger train before? I couldn't recall.) to the now demolished Ravenswood housing projects in Queens—wealthy Manhattanites, it seemed, didn't want the eyesore on their island anymore—there'd been a dash to buy up the property, with the entire block eventually being sold to a Taiwanese real estate company for an undisclosed amount. No one mourned the loss of Madison Square Garden. The sports teams that played there were consistently awful—basketball stars defecting to more lucrative leagues in China or Dubai—and many of the more popular musicians had begun giving concerts primarily via VR headset to save the money spent on touring.

I humped my bag through the Garment District, momentarily distracted by the aroma of Swedish Meatballs wafting out of the IKEA that occupied the ground floor of the New York Times Building. Could I run in and grab something to eat? I stuffed the thought away. Prioritizing sleep, I had neglected to change in the cramped Megabus bathroom and had only fifteen minutes to get in my gear and be in front of the service elevator with the rest of my team. The lifts ran on a tight schedule, free from leniency, and sending one back for a single tardy person was an expense not taken lightly. As such, if you missed it, Robison-Moon docked you half a day's pay, the apparent cost of operation plus a little extra as discipline.

I made my way beneath scads of ceaseless scaffolding, past the many vacant storefronts of former smoke shops. Vaping, like my beloved coin pushers, had come under new legislation in the last decade, and now the stores that sold vaporizer kits had to be operated "outside of the public consciousness." This meant that many stores had literally gone underground, servicing customers through stairwells that led under the sidewalk, little not-yet-illicit tunnels of sour-smelling haze.

Emerging from the scaffolding, I saw it: a monolith of glass panels that loomed high over the nearby structures, reflecting the intermittent blink of aircraft warning aerials atop the surrounding behemoths. A man-made object that, were you at the very top, would allow you to witness Earth's gentle curvature.

This was The Pinnacle, the world's tallest building by one hundred floors and rising. It was also where I had been working for the last eighteen months.

By the time I made my way around the demonstrators picketing near the worker entrance—there were always people protesting the construction; second and third-generation New Yorkers who disliked the idea of their city being made less filthy—I was having to pull my coveralls on as I walked, hopping from foot to foot as I struggled to get the leg cuffs over my boots. My team was just stepping onto the elevator, and I called out for Saeed to hold it as long as he could while I wrestled into my safety harness.

"If he misses it, he misses it," I heard Noor say. "We don't wait."

I was barely within reach when Saeed took my hand and pulled me inside. My breath was fire in my windpipe and it took everything in me to keep from hacking my lungs out in the cramped elevator car. Our crew of twenty-five filled the space completely, despite it being the size of my living room.

Noor shook her head and punched in the floor code with her knuckle, which she shielded from us with the flat of her hand.

Passing over the elevator gap that separated The Pinnacle and the rest of the world was a tense maneuver. The industrial doors closed at seemingly random intervals and with terrifying force. To hear them come together was to be reminded of the collision of speeding automobiles or the unexpected meeting of heavy magnets. A section of our onboarding was dedicated specifically to instruction on how to react to the doors, which, we were told, could easily sever an arm or leg. *Pick a side,* the horrifying safety video said. *In or out, but do not linger:* a repeated sentiment which was intercut with grisly reenactments of worksite injuries. To see a mannequin arm so fiercely amputated was deterrent enough. No one had ever heard of someone actually being injured by the doors themselves, but given the severity with which Robison-Moon described their danger, I wasn't aching to see what could happen.

I steadied myself for a moment so as to get one last view of the city before the doors closed, sealing us in The Pinnacle for what might now be eleven days. The sun thinned through the clouds slightly, rays of light illuminating a septic grate, an elderly Chinese couple passing a bottle of water between them, a boarded-up Duane Reade. The aroma of nuts roasted in imitation cinnamon wafted over from a cart across the street. Two disposable plastic bottles of urine clogged a storm drain. Pigeons congregated on a large spool of fiber-optic cable, conversing, or maybe serenading one another.

And then slowly, like theater curtains coming together at the end of an act, it all disappeared, and we were moving.

INITIALLY, The Pinnacle—code-named "Rock Candy" during the municipal approval process—consisted of only two-hundred stories, making it still unquestionably the tallest building on the planet. Designed for mixed-use with alternating floors of office space and condos, the expedited construction concluded in just over a year. Robison-Moon, the American-Korean company that won the building contract, staffed workers at every available hour; teams of a hundred on consecutive twelve-hour shifts. Not a single moment passed where the tower wasn't growing.

When the construction finished, the current building owners—it is said that initial ownership exchanged hands several times—who remained anonymous behind their Bahamian holding company and communicated only through a team of international lawyers, were pleased enough by the rapid progress that they drew up new plans which allowed for another fifty stories to be added to the top. Robison-Moon happily agreed, and the process began again. Without foundations to lay on the highest floors, the teams were pared down to twenty-five and the work slowed considerably. The dismissed employees— many of whom were laborers from developing countries stateside on fragile work visas—became valuable targets to journalists looking for details about the structure, if they could catch them before the deportation process began. Though Robison-Moon was nothing if not prepared, and the non-disclosure agreements we signed upon starting included words like *punitive, retaliatory,* and *severe retribution.* It felt as though their threats stopped just short of physical castigation.

It was after this turnover that I found myself employed by Robison-Moon, first on some of their smaller projects in New Jersey and then, after a year, on The Pinnacle. I was just off a job rewiring an assisted living home in New Haven. We'd been made to work around the occupants so that the facility managers could save money on finding temporary housing, our ladders straddling hospital beds, ceiling debris dusting countless old people playing cacophonic penny slots on their phones. Awful work, but at least they let us eat in the cafeteria for free. Accepting Robison-Moon's offer was easy, once I saw the pay.

When The Pinnacle's set of additional floors was in place, the building owners requested another fifty added; then, after that, yet another fifty. It was on that most recent fifty that I currently worked.

As a team, we were under no illusions that this round of additions would be the last and waited for the day when a message would arrive through our corporate email accounts—no doubt sandwiched between spam ads for weight-loss injectables and rideshare apps—that outlined the next stage of the building's already endless growth. Robison-Moon wouldn't deny the building owners their revision. The money, which a *Times* journalist discovered came in the form of cryptocurrency—thereby making it difficult to trace—was seemingly without end.

The minute-to-minute fabrication of The Pinnacle was nothing extraordinary, save its unprecedented scale. Sink a screw, grout tile, cut a recess for lighting. What was remarkable lay beyond what I or any of my coworkers had access to. To stabilize the structure and keep it from toppling in the event of some calamitous catastrophe, an enormous titanium rod—a material which, in recent years, eclipsed gold in price—had been run through its center and deep underground.

We called this rod The Spike. The details of its dimensions were not publicly available—Robison-Moon considered this a "trade secret"—but everyone on the jobsite wagered it to extend at least a mile below the surface. No one I knew had seen it in person—it was always secured behind a heavy and windowless metal door—but rumors were rampant, friends of friends saying that it was radioactive, that it tasted like sugarcane if licked, that it didn't even really exist.

It's made me sterile, a mason from another team had posted on Zone.

Don't you ride horses bareback? Saeed replied.

What's your point?

The team that assembled each new section of The Spike flew in from Ukraine and stayed on a floor separate from the rest of us. We only ever saw them at shift changes and were forbidden from speaking with them. They always looked so tired, shuffling from the elevator like zombies in hard hats.

Although nearly all of the completed floors were move-in ready, the building owner refused to let anyone lease space until the project was entirely finished, whatever that meant. As a result, the structure was eerily sterile, the vacant floors quiet save for the concrete and steel creaking under its own weight. The laborer's quarters were three stories below whatever floor was currently being worked on, complete with a small mess kitchen with microwaveable food and a rec room where we played cards or watched television. Everything was provided for us by the company, though at the cost of a certain amount of freedom: we weren't allowed to leave the building during the week we were on the clock and the windows on the floors in-progress were covered in a thick black plastic, another attempt on behalf of Robison-Moon to keep their construction methods private. We toiled under dim artificial light and refiltered air for seven straight days. When we finally took the elevator down on Sunday morning, Noor had to guide us through an exercise of gradually opening and closing our eyes so that the sun that accompanied the parting doors didn't fry our atrophied retinas. Perhaps our eyes would someday vanish completely without the sunlight to fill them, like those salamanders who spend the entirety of their lives in caves.

Saeed and I were both electricians, and together with a team of construction engineers, certified plumbers, and general contractors, we could complete a floor in about fourteen days with the help of automation. Materials came to us precut, walls already painted, screws, nails, and staples precisely counted. It was like putting together a puzzle more than anything else, pieces fitting together just so. Its ease made the work frequently boring. Thread a wire, ground a line, push a plastic housing into a lighting fixture. Eat, scroll, shit. Repeat for seven days then go home and sleep more than you ever have in your entire life.

And no drinking.

Get caught with any kind of booze, even something tangentially alcoholic like mouthwash, and you were fired immediately without severance and disqualified from receiving unemployment benefits. Our bags, left at the foot of our beds, were searched daily for contraband while we worked.

Divested of booze by Robison-Moon and its faceless affiliates, my off weeks had grown into seven-day binges. I'd start easy, a beer or two at lunch, then continue well into the night.

I had bottles stashed all over the house: behind the expired cough syrup in the vanity, in the pocket of a winter jacket hanging in the closet, nestled between sleeping bags amidst the camping gear. I'd sneak sips whenever I could and be far gone by sundown, stumbling around the house knocking picture frames from the walls in an attempt to make my way upstairs. To her credit, Embry tolerated this behavior longer than I would have were the roles reversed. The breaking point—perhaps the culmination of many smaller, though no less meaningful, breaking points—had come three months ago, when I woke up facedown in the couch cushions on a particularly awful morning-after. Embry sat in the chair opposite the couch, flipping through an old issue of *American Philatelist* her sister had left behind. Beneath her right eye was a smear of purple.

"I didn't do that, did I?" I propped myself up on the couch and suppressed the urge to vomit.

"No. Well, yes. Not how you mean."

In a drunken attempt to sweep Embry off her feet and carry her over the bedroom threshold—something, I wagered, she had protested—I accidentally smacked her face against the doorframe. This, of course, bothered me greatly, not only because I had injured the woman I loved very much, but that I couldn't recall doing it.

I sat up and sipped coffee that had clearly been poured several hours ago. I was then given an ultimatum: either stop drinking or find somewhere else to live. The choice was easy: I would quit drinking. Toward this goal I had only gone halfway, still enjoying a beer or three and the occasional swig of hard liquor, though now in moderation and entirely in secret. When I was at Canteen—a place that felt comfortable in its discomfort—I told Embry I was running errands, so when I actually had errands I had to run them when she was out with friends or working so as to hide my lie.

I haven't been truly drunk since that morning. Well-oiled sure, and buzzed most certainly, but never the kind of plastered like before, singing my dinner to the inside of the toilet bowl and then trying to kiss Embry with lips slick from bile.

And that, I believed, was progress.

My father pushed for institutional help, for meetings.

"Find people. Start from there," he told me, nursing Dr Pepper from a rocks glass on our back patio. The sunset was especially vibrant due to the exhaust coming from a nearby ethanol plant. He'd helped me assemble a shed, yet another project in my insatiable appetite for home renovation.

"I dunno," I replied. "It feels like being at church."

"You know this from experience?"

"I've seen it on television."

Sitting there with him, I was already envisioning the places in the shed I could secret away alcohol: in the half-empty fertilizer bag, beneath an upturned wheelbarrow, in work gloves unoccupied by spiders.

"It's not so bad, really."

This was the first I'd heard of my father's problems with alcohol. I couldn't recall ever having seen him drink, so I pressed him for more.

"This was before you were born, of course. A year or so after your mom and I got married. It was her that marched me down there, actually. Told me I could get fixed or fix to leave." He stared off at the horizon dotted with Port Authority cranes and idly ran his hand over a surgical scar across his sternum. "And I wasn't sober that first time."

"You weren't?"

"I was on the tail end of something. Vodka, maybe, from the night before. Your mother drove me to the nearest meeting, a yoga studio in the strip mall down by the styrofoam plant. She sat in the parking lot for an hour. I came back to the car with donuts in both pockets. 'They didn't give you anything? Like, a coin or a keychain?' she asked me."

"What'd you tell her?"

He told me that if he was going down that road, really going down it, then he should at least be sober for that first meeting. So they went again the next day and he got his chip.

"How many times did you go?"

"Enough. I still do, sometimes, if things feel hard. All this started a year or so after my dad died."

His father, my grandfather, had crashed his car coming up the coast road from Stamford, died upon impact. He'd no doubt been drinking. I'd never get the chance to meet him.

"What started it all?" That there were things about my father that I had yet to learn, that I may never learn were he to die, was destabilizing. I thought about asking him more, about excavating further, but a rift had opened in my familiarity, the two sides of which represented knowing as much as I could and knowing as little as I could. After all, what else could emerge?

"How it came upon me I can't say I know. I suppose some people just start and never can seem to stop."

I didn't respond to this. I also didn't tell him what I read online, that alcoholism was an inherited disease, that a coin had been flipped at my birth, and at my father's birth, and at his father's birth, about whether our genes would be knit through with addiction.

Many of the other people on the jobsite clearly had similar compulsions, the deprivation of which led to new avenues for dependency. The vending machine in the mess was consistently out of sugar soda and sunflower seeds. There was gambling at all hours, card games and dominoes and European football broadcast via satellite. At lights-out there was an underlying hum of masturbation.

My coping mechanism manifested itself in an unyielding weeklong jones. No matter what I was doing, the thought ran through my brain in the background like the buzz of fluorescent lighting, imagining the first drink I would have when I returned to earth, so to speak. Didn't I deserve that? Just one drink after a long week at work? After clearing the elevator doors I would find a bar somewhere in Midtown and order something that came in a large glass. And with each drink I'd think, *maybe this will be the last cold beer I ever have,* but by the end of that thought my glass would be empty, another placed in my hand, and as I drank that new beer, I would think, *maybe this will be the last cold beer I ever have.*

Overall, working on The Pinnacle was a pretty good gig, and it beat digging irrigation canals in the blueberry fields around New Haven, a career to which my brother had long ago resigned himself. My father, despite his protestations at my not having a safe desk job, was at least happy I made use of my degree, and my mother enjoyed that I wasn't still living at home. Even Embry, despite how she felt about my being away so often, had begun to tell her friends about my job as though it were something that carried a cultural cachet, that we were part of something big, saying that I worked on "that super-secret building in the city."

Those close to me were in the minority when it came to public opinion on The Pinnacle. Republicans hated the cost; Democrats hated the mysterious backers; environmentalists hated the pollution caused by the construction; Manhattanites hated the newly obstructed skyline; and academics hated the project for more philosophical reasons.

"Frankly," Dr. Helmut Stedhoffer, chair of sociology at Columbia University, said to an NPR correspondent, "they are building a contemporary Tower of Babel, one that could very well meet a similar fate."

The *New York Post* had less erudite thoughts on the project, calling it "The Big Apple's Brand-New Glistening Penis."

"Penis or no, at least there's food on your plate," my father said, handing me a glass-bottle Coke. And there would be, until the project was done at least, which may not be in my lifetime or the lifetime of the generation after mine. Coin flip after coin flip.

"Amen," I replied, and we clinked glasses.

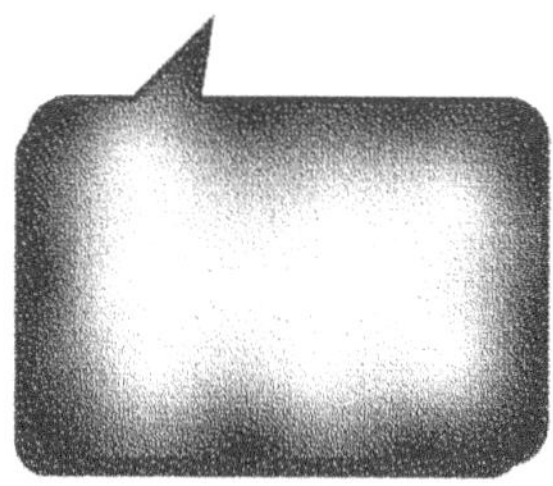

"ANY word on what's going on?" Embry asked.

"Nothing yet." We'd just gotten released from our first shift: a short two-hour affair to get back on schedule. Saeed and I spent the entire time installing baseboard electrical outlets, a fairly routine task that left my back on fire. "Everything seems normal."

I leaned my head against the wall and cradled the handset between my neck and shoulder. Cell service was—perhaps intentionally—non-existent in the barracks, so instead we used a bank of landlines bolted to the wall to communicate with the outside world. Every six hours we were allotted three minutes to speak with whomever we wanted. Though no kindness, however small, went without suspicion, and there was the strong sense that someone was listening to our phone calls and selling our private conversations to marketing agencies.

"How'd the portrait turn out?"

"They're never satisfied." I could hear something sizzling on the stovetop through the receiver. "People don't like seeing themselves through the eyes of others."

A series of beeps alerted me that I only had thirty seconds left on the call before it would hang up automatically. A queue had formed behind me; other men eager for their metered minutes.

I told Embry I loved her and hung up the receiver. I cleaned the handset with a sanitizing wipe plucked from a wall-mounted box and then tossed said wipe atop a growing pile on the floor.

Truth was I hadn't told Embry everything, a recurring theme in our relationship. When my team arrived on the 324th floor there was already a crew present: guards armed with automatic weapons rather than construction laborers. Noor instructed us to not interact with them, to give as much space as possible. She would answer no further questions.

Along the middle of the floor, a plywood partition had been hastily assembled to shield The Spike's menacing metal door. Through this barrier the guards moved in and out using a single-person-wide opening between the panels behind which I thought I could make out a faint whirring sound. While little was known about The Spike, it was clear that it created a high-frequency whine that sometimes escaped from the chamber in which it was housed. Though the noise I had just heard was somehow different: deeper, more resonant, as though something heavy were spinning very slowly.

Our team was stationed at the opposite end of the jobsite, and as soon as we completed our work for the day Noor rushed us into the elevator and down to our quarters. For the rest of the night the elevators ran constantly, always stopping at the floor we had been working on and whooshing back down to the ground shortly after. The regularity at which they moved emulated a heartbeat, the *whumphing* past our quarters a steady contraction and release.

I neglected to tell Embry this not because of the countless short films and emails we received about self-censorship—who knows what details about the jobsite were privileged and which were not—but because I didn't want to worry her unnecessarily. After all, The Pinnacle was a giant unknown, and I was sure that many unexplained things happened within it, things that, if I were to become privy to them, could get me fired, or worse. I was not immune to thinking that the entire building had a sinister quality, something dark lurking behind the reflective window glass on the many unoccupied floors.

Particles of that darkness occasionally made themselves known. To the general public this manifested in anomalies visible from the outside: a single illuminated light on one of the floors, its glow like a baleful eye, or a seemingly unending stream of yellow steam billowing from pipes situated around the base of the structure. The Pinnacle's mere existence fueled a macabre curiosity for many. After all, how could something so massive, so without any conceivable comparison, be constructed without some associated awfulness? Upon learning of my involvement with the construction, a friend of Embry's posted multiple times on social media, tagging me over images of cramped workers in a Mongolian copper mine, of mass, unmarked graves beside Dubai's newest monolith.

I perceived it all through a less interesting lens. This was just a job for me, and whose job wasn't at least in some tangential way connected to something disquieting? That's what I told myself, anyway.

Though the disappearance of the other crew and the appearance of the armed personnel in their place did seat in me a certain menace that felt less abstract and more stick and blood and bone.

I didn't want to sleep just yet, so I wandered into the mess, where Saeed sat alone at one of the long tables, hunched over his phone, no doubt scrolling through Zone. I settled into a space across from him and fidgeted with a deck of cards someone had left behind.

"There's a lot of chatter," Saeed said. He took a screenshot, then another. Zone came through on our phones with amazing speed and clarity while other apps floundered, no doubt by design. "Look at this."

Saeed slid his phone across the table. A post was loaded up showing a photo of two guards, the same we had seen earlier, loading long black bags into the back of an armored car.

"Who took that?" I asked.

"Someone on Kirsch's crew who lives in the city. I captured it as soon as I could. Good thing, too, because now it's gone."

"They deleted the photo?"

"More like they deleted their entire account."

We allowed this information to sit between us for a moment.

"You don't think..." I began but couldn't finish the thought, letting it linger like a toxic cloud.

"No. No, they would have told us about something like that, I'm sure of it."

"Would they?" Workplace accidents weren't uncommon, especially in construction. "I mean, if the entire other crew had died, if there had been a gas leak or a ceiling collapse or—"

Saeed made a serious face, opening his eyes wide as though to tell me to stop talking.

The level to which we were monitored was never abundantly clear, but we assumed that something was listening to us at nearly every moment. We'd receive targeted ads through Zone based on things we'd been talking about in passing. At times it felt as though the scope of their surveillance went beyond even that, as though they were listening in on our thoughts and projecting our desires back at us through our phone screens. *Hadn't I always wanted a smartwatch,* I would think as a coupon for one popped into my Zone DMs.

I pulled the playing cards from their box and began to shuffle simply to give my hands something to do. My father said this urge to have my fingers constantly occupied was a byproduct of drinking less. The cards were patterned with deepfake images of nude celebrities, their faces imposed upon the bodies of internet sex workers.

I belched into my closed mouth and the memory of beer from earlier flooded my tongue. The taste made me want more, a few cans, maybe even a six-pack.

"I really want a drink," Saeed said, placing his phone facedown on the table in a rare instance of digital abstention. Had he read my mind?

Ever empathetic to another's desire for liquor, I pulled an imaginary bottle from beneath the table and opened it with an imaginary church key before pouring imaginary lager into an imaginary glass. I slid this invisible libation toward Saeed before repeating the process for myself.

We exchanged an unenthusiastic *cheers* and downed the phantom contents in one long pull.

A small tube television—a model that predated my birth by at least a decade—sat playing in one of the mess's corners and Saeed and I watched a show where a man, stranded by his own design in the Siberian wilderness, survived only on what sustenance he could find in the snow-covered forest. An emaciated rabbit caught in a snare bit the man's hand as he attempted to break its neck and scampered away, drops of blood dotting the front of his camouflage pants. The closed captions read [INAU-DIBLE] though his frustrations were clear by the way his mouth formed the word "fuck" so many times. Nothing, it seemed, was coming easy to anyone.

"You're not curious?" I finally asked.

"Of course I am." Saeed picked up his phone, his brief internet fast broken, and dove back into Zone. "But what good comes from curiosity?"

I asked Saeed if there had been any more posts about the armed guards and the bags.

"None. It may as well not have happened."

"Maybe it didn't." At this Saeed looked up at me, his face slack from exhaustion. Though I'd been witness to many deceptions by those in power over the last few decades, I realized that my experiences were in no way comparable to those that The Pinnacle's many immigrant laborers had endured in their home countries, where labor laws came secondary to progress. In this paradigm I could write off the sudden changes at the jobsite, the urgent need for new bodies. After all, what's the worst that could have happened? This was still America, and that, I believed, was a kind of shield.

Suddenly, something on the floor above shook our ceiling as though a great weight had been dropped, causing bits of acoustic tile dust to fall on the table between us.

We acknowledged the sound, the feeling, by making eye contact, but said nothing further about it. These kinds of events, The Pinnacle convulsing as though electrified, were frequent. The team working in the mirror image of our own—who slept during the daylight on a different floor and then toiled in the night hours and whom, I'm sure, I had never seen outside of Zone by design—had probably dropped a piece of cement board or shifted a pallet off its rolling platform. Anything could make a noise like that, really. It wasn't worth worrying over. Well, usually. Uncertainty has a way of amplifying the imagination, though, of making monsters out of shadows cast by the space where walls come together.

Saeed brushed the particles onto the floor and continued to browse Zone, interrupted only by the overhead lights flashing on and off, a signal from the company that it was time to go to bed.

Saeed unplugged the television from the wall—there was no way to turn it off properly as the power button had been sealed over with resin—and we made our way to the row of beds located near the large, enclosed cylinder where we knew The Spike to spin. Its proximity resulted in a constant warmth. We had been assured that this heat bore no immediate risk to our health. Saeed had asked for that same assurance in writing, though if he ever got it, he hadn't told us about it. Beside my bed a poster with only a large letter "E" hung on the wall, the direction of Mecca from New York City.

"My father wanted me to be a podiatrist," Saeed said. We were pulling clean sheets over our mattresses. The first night was always the worst, everyone writhing and turning, trying to recreate the feeling of sleeping at home, its specific contours.

"A foot doctor?"

"It's a position of high regard. Even the ancient Egyptians knew that."

"Why didn't you go for it?"

"I couldn't handle the sight of blood. There's no way I'd have made it through medical school. My father was crushed, of course, when I told him I was going to be an engineer. I think he wanted to be the kind of person who could say 'my son, the doctor' when talking to his friends."

If my father wanted me to follow any specific path, he hadn't made it known. When he heard how I decided to make my living, the proximity to tools and to fabrication and construction, he appeared deflated, as though it were too closely adjacent to his own line of work, which he seemed so desperate to escape through his next astounding invention. There was a television show that aired on basic cable growing up where inventors pitched their ideas to a group of venture capitalists, an opportunity my father salivated at. Very infrequently did these contestants look like they could be successful, and the mere idea that they had to stand while the ultra-wealthy could sit in their padded swivel chairs made the whole process seem like a joke at their expense. He's still working, my father, thirty hours a week shouldering drywall panels around and digging out compound dust from the folds of his elbows and knees.

I tucked the final corner of my sheets beneath the mattress. They were our backup set at home, bleach-stained and frayed. "Is there a lot of blood in podiatry?"

"More than in electrical engineering." Saeed sat on his bed and pulled out his phone. After sunset the lights in the barracks were dimmed by half to emulate the outside world, which gave everyone a sallow, malnourished appearance. The light from Saeed's phone accentuated this further; he looked like a corpse.

It used to be that you didn't need a degree to be an electrician, but the apprenticeship program nationwide had all but collapsed when the Baby Boomers died out. Now, the only way to get training was to go to school, to amass debt.

"Hey, this is whose?" Ilyas, one of the HVAC specialists, pointed to a piece of rolling luggage near the foot of his bed. When no one responded, he read out the name written on a piece of duct tape stretched across its side. "Rabinoux?"

We all recognized the name. He was one of the glaziers on the crew we were replacing. His posts on Zone, of the classic cars he restored in his free time, were legendary.

"Do you think he forgot?" I asked Saeed.

"Would you?"

The suitcase, a red-and-black soft-body with the Dodge logo stenciled onto the front, looked normal enough, but an imaginary forcefield seemed to emit from it and no one dared get close. I felt like we should have talked about what to do with it, but instead we all just stared at one another until Ilyas pushed it to the center of the room with the handle of a broom, where it sat like a wart.

When the lights went off—automatically at nine—we were uncharacteristically quiet, the usual whispered conversations between neighbors pushed back into the caverns of our bodies. Then, one by one, we winked into sleep, 300 floors up in what a New York Department of Labor Safety and Worker Protection report once called, "not yet a massive deathtrap."

By morning the suitcase was gone.

EVERY year, my father endeavored to make my birthday and Christmas presents himself. He would take the station wagon on a tour of his usual haunts—the Yale Engineering College Surplus Store, Everyday Thrift on Taylor Street, the IKEA dumpster—and return with plastic grocery bags of raw and discarded materials. The resulting gifts were always far removed from what I had asked for. In response to hearing I wanted a Nintendo, I received instead a foosball table—clearly used—with the little plastic players swapped out for crude versions of knights and dragons made from a cut up old hood vent, burred edges sharp to the touch, and a steel bearing in place of the ball. After requesting a new monitor for my computer, a large rectangular box appeared beneath the tree. Naively assuming I knew what was inside I tore through the wrapping paper only to be greeted by a wall clock with the hands replaced by a gold-plated knife and fork. After my twelfth birthday, my mother would pull me aside while my father was at work and ask me point-blank what gifts I really wanted. She would then buy them, unbeknownst to my father, and give them to me in secret. Throughout the following year, as my father went about the house, he would inquire about my new boots or headphones.

"When did you get those?" he would ask, searching his memory.

And I would lie and tell him that I was picking up extra jobs mowing lawns around the neighborhood to earn money. As caring as my father was, his attention was consistently elsewhere, and he accepted what I told him unquestioningly.

On my eighteenth birthday, the last I would be living at home, he gave me the crowning achievement of his craftsmanship. Inside of a slice of store-bought birthday cake he had hidden a key, which I discovered with one of my molars.

"Hmmm," he said, rubbing his chin in faux surprise, "I wonder what that could be for?"

I allowed myself to be led out to the driveway, where, in place of the station wagon, sat an unassuming red Honda. It had clouded headlights, rust rimming the wheel wells, and paint peeling off in large patches like a body beset with sores. It was at least fifty years old, based on the angular frame and beige upholstery, which I could just see through a windshield laced with cracks.

"Well? What do you think?" My father stepped out in front and sat on the hood, his hands spread wide as though showing off his greatest treasure.

What could I say? I hadn't been asking for a car, but my father, who saw The American Dream as a series of rungs on an attainable ladder, believed that car ownership was one of the tenets of adulthood. And wasn't I an adult now? If he only knew how accelerated my path to this state had been: the drinking at friends' houses, the fistfights on school property, the copious unprotected sex. That I was lying to him, to protect him from my newly absent innocence, felt like a boosted level of maturity, one that felt uncomfortable and weighted. As far as my father was concerned, this gift—this exact moment—was my emergence from a pupal stage. I could now be regarded among all the other men in his life. I had arrived and would be doing so from that point forward in a car that looked as though it had been fished from the bottom of a lake.

My brother—who had been the recipient of many previous and similarly well-intentioned gifts—elbowed me hard in the ribs. "Tell him you love it," he whispered.

So I did, and like an excited child my father grabbed my hand and dragged me to the car, guiding me on a tour of all its wonderful features, which, in reality, were simply aspects of every car that had ever been made. "Look!" he said, motioning. "It's so easy to open the trunk!"

When the tour finished, he instructed me to sit behind the wheel so that he could take a photo. Returning with his phone he also told me to put on my letter jacket, which he had retrieved from my closet. I'd lettered in academics, but all my father cared about was what the jacket represented: success in that most American of institutions.

The car was unlike any other gift my father had ever given me. It appeared to have no odd tinkering or busted plastic through which he'd accidentally run his power drill. Most kids would see it as a way out, a token of freedom. Though in truth I was never overly bound by my mother or father. I had no curfew and could come and go as I pleased if my grades were good, which I ensured they were if not simply for this privilege.

"Now let me show you the kicker," my father said, gesturing for me to come around to the hood. He popped it open, and a wave of acrid, burnt-smelling air came rushing out. It was as though an animal had become trapped within the chassis and died. "This, right here," my father said, tapping on the engine block, "runs entirely on used vegetable oil. I rigged it up myself."

There it was, his stamp.

"I talked with a couple of the restaurants in town, and they said they'd give you their wastage for free." He was beaming. This was perhaps the moment he had most anticipated since learning that he was going to be a father.

I hugged him, of course I did, and said a profuse number of thank yous before he had me turn the engine over to make sure it was working. The car eventually coughed to life and for the rest of the day my clothes smelled like french fries.

I drove that car only when necessary and the embarrassment I felt pouring depleted kitchen grease into my gas tank in the back alley of Cary's Chicken Sandwiches was immeasurable. As such, after I moved out, I kept the car in a friend's backyard utility shed, taking it out only when visiting so that my father could look upon his handiwork. When he knew I was close to the house—the smell a portent of my arrival—he would stand on the porch and watch as I pulled into the driveway beside the station wagon, his pride a bright beacon.

The car is scrap metal now, of course. It was never designed to run on cooking oil and whatever kitchen table engineering my father did was probably cobbled together from internet videos and a generally assumed idea that he just "understood" how things worked.

Even now he brings up the car when I visit.

"That was really something, wasn't it? Do you remember that car? Could outlast anything else on the road, I wager. Vegetable oil or not, that sure was something."

I'm not sure I deserved the gift, looking back. I was cruel to my parents in the way that all teenagers are, resentful of their mere presence in my life. I recall more than one occasion where I called my father a "fucking asshole" in response to not being allowed to have friends over or after refusing to spend Sunday morning at my grandmother's nursing home because I was secretly hungover. My father's love, I realized only much later, while perhaps a bit misguided, was completely unconditional, and now whenever I smell fry oil I am reminded of that car and the way that, on hot spring days, the entire neighborhood would reek of hash browns upon my arrival home from school.

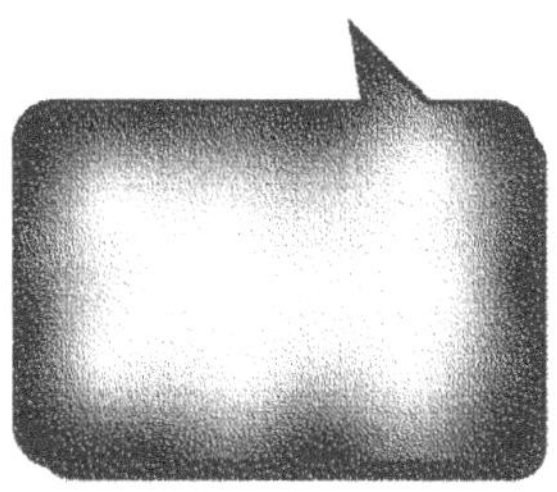

SAEED and I spent the first full shift on-site installing fiber-optic cable. With all we'd run through The Pinnacle so far, we wagered that Robison-Moon had spent close to fifteen million on the cable alone. Given the high cost of it, among other materials, Robison-Moon had brought in a fleet of Automated Measuring Apparatuses— essentially a robotic vacuum with a laser level taped to it—to calculate the exact amount we'd need down to the millimeter. We'd be securing wire to run alongside a steel divider and the little guys would rover between our legs, beeping conversation to one another. It was like having a litter of mechanical puppies at the jobsite.

We'd taken to giving them names, the ten AMAs our team had been allotted, differentiated by a piece of colored tape placed on their battery covers. That day it happened to be Ponshu—a Americanization of pączusiu, a word meaning "little donut" given to it by Piotr, the Polish mason who laid tile—that was following diligently behind as we routed cable through the drop ceiling tiles, beeping while relaying data to the server array located at street level in an industrial shipping container.

"Hand me those needle-nose," Saeed said, his head hidden within the network of supports that held up the ceiling.

"It's staring at me."

"What is?"

"Ponshu." Identified by a band of golden masking tape, the robot was no larger than my dog back in New Haven. It had been hanging out near me all day while I worked, forcing me to take big steps to avoid crushing it beneath my boots. As I steadied the ladder upon which Saeed was balanced, I could see Ponshu's infrared camera pointed up at me, tracking my face.

"You're imagining things. It's probably just getting caught on something glinting off your glasses." As Saeed said this, Ponshu pushed itself against my foot and I nudged it away several times before it stayed put.

It wasn't until the end of the day, when an inaudible high frequency ping called all the AMAs to return to their charging bay, that Ponshu finally left me alone. As it retreated, I watched its small plastic wheels navigate over shards of drywall and angle iron. When its tread got jammed up on someone's discarded hammer, I almost ran to set it right, as one would a young child learning to crawl. But we weren't supposed to touch them. It could damage the fragile, and very expensive internal sensors, so I turned my back on Ponshu and let it learn on its own how to best free itself. The same technology that went into Ponshu had been historically implemented in military drones, and in remembering this I imagined the little robot with a grenade taped to its front slowly rolling into combat.

At the elevator there was new security. Before we were allowed to board, two men with Robison-Moon security badges forced us to empty our pockets and remove our shoes and socks. They patted down the entirety of our bodies before waving something that looked like a black-light over our faces, lingering for a moment on our eyes.

"Don't worry," Noor told us. "There is no need to worry. But please, no questions. Don't worry."

We knew something was wrong, but we also knew

that saying so would result in Noor taking us in for a lecture on how hurt she felt that we didn't trust her, our diligent supervisor.

I'd never done anything at work that resulted in discipline, perhaps due to the lack of alcohol on-site. I understood that losing my job was not in my best interest. Robison-Moon paid well, and there existed at the periphery an idea that the construction of The Pinnacle may never cease, which meant paychecks for as long as I wanted them.

Of course I was privileged. I would only lose my job should something happen. Others on my team weren't as lucky; they could be deported with little notice, year-long Manhattan leases wasted on the roaches that had steadily grown in population over the last five years.

When it was my turn at the elevator doors, I was instructed to open my eyes as wide as possible as the light passed over them.

"Will this hurt?" I shot a glance at Noor, and she scrunched her face up in response.

We'd known from the night before that something wasn't right at the jobsite. When we had come up this morning the floor had been hastily cleaned, with materials propped against one another and the residue from powder-actuated tools swept into piles. There were footprints everywhere, crossing over and doubling back, movement at double speed. One of the Egyptian glaziers discovered a lone work glove beneath a heap of discarded paper tape. He held it delicately with his thumb and index finger, away from his body as though there were a hand still inside of it. Two of the armed guards took it from him and retreated to the elevator where they began a whispered argument before being silenced by the closing doors.

The handheld beam passed slowly over my face, and as tears formed at the edges of my eyes, I was forced to keep my lids open with the tips of my fingers. It felt as though the guards were looking for something, scanning methodically, all the while taking notes on a tablet attached to their belts. The flesh of my face felt unnaturally warm, like I had been suspended over a pot of boiling water. I couldn't shake the feeling that I was being somehow sterilized. While waiting for the rest of the laborers to receive their unexplained treatment, I followed the many floaters left behind in my vision. Long and sinuous, they darted in and out of my field of view, resistant to capture. They patterned the plywood divider that had been erected through the center of the floor like animated graffiti, forming what looked like arrows pointing toward the entrance to The Spike. I asked Saeed if he was experiencing something similar and he said no.

As a child, maybe ten or eleven, I spent the bulk of an entire afternoon staring up at the sky through a blanket of thin clouds. I could just make out the sun's outline, as though it were shrouded behind an impossibly large bedsheet and followed its arc toward the horizon. When it began to get cold, somewhere close to evening, I stood up and discovered a large amorphous circle in the middle of my vision, its edges moving like an amoeba on a microscope slide. That night, at dinner, the circle remained, obscuring the entirety of the dinner table as I mistakenly poured Italian dressing over my mashed potatoes instead of gravy.

"Are you high?" my mother asked.

I told her that I wasn't, really, but was too ashamed to admit the real reason for my odd behavior. Had my father been eating with us—instead of in the garage burning his own retinas by welding without a mask—he would have told my mother she was being ridiculous. This boy, he would have said, he's just an odd duck, is all. He would have then made a quacking noise that never failed to make my brother and I laugh uncontrollably.

Finally crammed into the elevator, we were overtaken

by an uncomfortable silence. We wanted to talk about what just happened, but with Noor beside us, plus the unknown surveillance in the car itself, we kept silent, staring at our shoes or counting the seconds between floors. When we finally parted ways—Noor remaining on the elevator as she made her way down to the women's barracks—we all brought out our phones and began to prowl through Zone, searching for anything at all out of the ordinary.

The app, however, was completely sanitized, many of the most recent posts scrubbed regardless of their content or source. In their place was an endless stream of algorithmically-generated ads. Mine in particular promised a better night's sleep with an adjustable mattress as well as discounted hourly rates on addiction therapy, both clearly results of eavesdropped conversations between Embry and myself.

A message came over the loudspeaker informing us that our pre-packaged dinners wouldn't be made available for another hour, and with little left to do in the meantime we gathered around the television and watched the last minutes of an uneventful EuroLeague basketball game.

"Are we gonna talk about it?" Aarav, one of the junior jobsite engineers, ratcheted up his recliner and muted the television.

Some of the men who had been working on the project for longer, who had worked for Robison-Moon on other megastructures—the World Cup stadium in Lagos, the bridges that now linked the Hawaiian islands—glared at him, their eyebrows raised, then made a show of looking up at the ceiling.

"You all are paranoid. They can't punish us for talking about it." Aarav was dewy, fresh out of college in Mumbai. All of his gear was still pristine, bereft of tears or gouges. Yet, because of his advanced degree, we all assumed he made a good deal of money. More, perhaps, than some of the old-timers who had been at it for years. Some of them had even begun working on The Pinnacle when the space was still occupied by Madison Square Garden. Piotr had a photo on his phone showing a torn-out piece of hard maple flooring that had the original half-court emblem for the New York Knicks painted upon it. The next photo showed it framed behind glass in his cousin's garage out in Hempstead.

"Isn't that looting?" I'd asked after he showed me.

"Does it matter now?"

Saeed, who had been fruitlessly scrolling, took the remote control from Aarav and turned the volume up on the television to an uncomfortable degree.

"Listen," Parth, an HVAC specialist, said, "whether or not we can talk about it doesn't mean we should, at least not out in the open like that."

We strained to hear Parth as he spoke to Aarav over the sound of a commercial extolling the virtues of probiotic yogurt. "Speculating about it is gonna get us all fired, don't think for a second that you're not replaceable."

Aarav's face was a combination of horror and disgust, the bluntness by which Parth was teaching him how the world worked was clearly an entirely new sensation. Parth made a face as though to ask if Aarav understood and in response Aarav nodded. Saeed returned the television volume to normal, and we all watched the final seconds of the game devolve into a series of meaningless free throws.

I was, perhaps, one of the luckier men on the jobsite. There had been a second wave of white flight about a decade ago, this time not from geographies but professions, and much of the blue-collar work had been left relatively unmanned. In response, many companies turned to sourcing their workforce from places like Pakistan and India, where the population was still rising and becoming more highly educated. The jobs these men held in the States were tenuous, though, and if anything went wrong there was no guarantee that you would be allowed to stay in the country.

Most came over as bachelors, with those who had families leaving them behind and sending money home. The men who brought their partners or children were seen as fools by the rest of the crew. To get a big enough apartment? To put your kids in school? To be tethered and take root? It was too easy to get fired, then deported. To Robison-Moon, we were all disposable. There was no infraction too small. Who, after all, wasn't looking for work? Because of this, the immigrant workers did everything they could to keep their jobs, refraining from most anything that could get them into trouble: recreational drugs, political demonstrations—even speeding. If I lost my job the worst that would happen is a trip to the unemployment office and a battery of paperwork that could be conquered in the better part of an afternoon if I were sober. Even so, it was distressing that you could be picked up and moved so easily like files between folders on a computer screen and plonked into the trash.

Thinking about it made me really want a drink.

"I'm going to hit the head," Piotr said as the final buzzer screeched on the television. He stood up and made a show of stretching out his back and arms.

At this, a few of the other men—Parth, Henry, a carpenter who I knew from a previous job, and some of the Indian laborers—said that they would accompany him, and together they retreated to the shared bathroom. It seemed an odd thing to do, but no one was paying much attention, engrossed instead by a promo for a police procedural on television taking place within a neon-lit strip club, PG-13 tits everywhere.

Uninterested, Saeed rose up and walked over to the beds at the far end of the barracks, separated from the rest of the space by a folding plastic partition. The entire living area was constructed like this; temporary walls, cardboard bed frames, and a layer of disposable linoleum over the carpet so that, when we moved with the building's growth, any evidence of our presence could be easily dismantled and replaced by a series of office cubicles or split into apartments. This left everything feeling exceptionally flimsy, and sound traveled so easily though the thin walls that, were we not routinely exhausted, sleep would be impossible.

I followed Saeed and sat on the mattress beside his own, watching as he folded and refolded a pair of gym shorts. The space on the other side of Saeed's bed had been empty for the last month, the man who had inhabited it having injured himself with a flooring nailer. We all envied the breathing room Saeed had gained. I was fortunate enough to sleep against the wall.

"I'm supposed to be upstate, Finger Lakes. Alex and I rented a cabin."

I sighed in sympathy.

"Right on Seneca. I should be there, right now, in a deck chair, watching fish jump out of the water."

"Did you cancel?" I asked.

"Couldn't. So Alex is going up with some friends from college. I didn't want it to go to waste."

He kept saying that name, Alex, as though it were a known entity between us. But in truth I didn't even know if Alex was a man or a woman, his wife, a girlfriend, or some companion he'd met online. I realized in that moment how little I knew Saeed at all outside of what he posted on Zone. I knew that he lived in Astoria, that he was agnostic, and that he had, in a story he told me once, accidentally burned off his eyebrows while attempting to fix a furnace, which is why they now grew patchy and uneven in color. He was an American citizen, born in New Canaan of all places. His brother had played high school football against my own. I felt especially bad because Saeed seemed to remember so much of what I told him about my own life, always asking after Embry and her projects, my parents, my progress on slowly remodeling the house. Perhaps I just wasn't a good listener, but in considering this a graver idea formed in my mind, the idea that I simply didn't care about hearing what others had to say, that I was selfish and negligent. At a certain point in my life, I accepted friends' invitations to bars only for the prospect of getting drunk, their conversation simply a formality on my way to killing brain cells with Kentucky Gentleman. But here, in this sober environment, literally walled off from temptation, the same problematic behaviors were finding purchase, and that scared me. For the second time that evening, I found myself desperately wanting a drink.

And then, as though to prove my point, I discovered that Saeed had been talking about something and asked me if I agreed.

"Totally," I said, not having any idea what I was supporting.

I told Saeed that I needed to use the restroom, though this was simply an excuse to extract myself from the conversation to which I had been barely listening. I was ashamed.

The group sitting before the television was now watching a reality show where someone's most prized possessions were either saved or destroyed based on their aptitude in tests of physical fitness. A woman watched in horror as a grand piano was dropped from a crane and exploded on the ground.

As I pushed through the bathroom door I happened upon a group of men, the same men who had left to use the restroom earlier, sitting on the tile, facing one another in a tight circle.

"What are you—"

The men turned their heads quickly in my direction and I could see Parth in the process of hiding something behind his back.

"Door! Shut!" Piotr hissed, then put a finger to his lips before waving me over.

It was an odd scene, the grown men in their wool work socks, seated like young children at primary school. They made space for me and I sat, unsure of what else to do. Piotr scared me. Rumor was that in his native Poland he'd been convicted of attempting to murder his landlord after a rent dispute. He dwarfed all of the other men on-site by at least four inches. He could snap a two-by-four over his knee; I'd seen it. Even seated on the floor he commanded attention, kneading his thick hands together.

I folded my legs beneath my body and rested on my palms. The floor was slightly sticky from what I hoped was only dried mop water.

"You won't tell anyone, will you?" Piotr poked his finger into the tender space just below my collarbone. I shook my head no simply to stop him from doing it again. In the morning, I would have a bruise.

Piotr nodded to Parth, who revealed a half-gallon lidded glass jar resting on the floor behind him. Three-quarters full with rust-colored liquid, bits of fruit peel floated near the bottom of the mixture. He screwed off the lid and instantly a bitter, astringent smell filled the room, overpowering the aroma of bleach and piss that had been present before. Parth passed the jar to Piotr, cradling it carefully as one would a newborn child, and Piotr handed it to me. The smell, so much closer now, brought tears to my eyes, and I had to stop myself from coughing in response to the severe odor which lit the back of my throat on fire.

Piotr mimed bringing the jar to his lips, but I needed no instruction. My eyes were already closed and the rim of the jar—warm from other mouths—collided sharply with my teeth, followed by a rush of stinging liquid down my throat.

It was perhaps the strongest liquor I'd ever consumed.

The taste, a combination of turpentine and pomegranate, gouged an unpleasant trench down toward my stomach, but the sensation of drinking was so instantly recognizable. My entire body sang and burned simultaneously. When I finally opened my eyes again they spun in my skull, the restroom set into motion atop a ball bearing. I was here, miles above the earth, miles from home, drinking homemade liquor from a canning jar not unlike the ones my grandmother preserved tomato sauce in.

It was the 21st century and it was briefly wonderful.

I prepared myself to take another sip, but Piotr took the glass and passed it around the circle, each man getting a turn. I could tell who was dependent and who was not based on how they drank. Those whose insides were already pickled by alcohol took the mixture down easily, savoring the way that their stomachs, empty from having dinner delayed, filled solely with booze. Then there were those, like Henry, who shuddered at the taste, the liquor a knife dragged through their body. Lightweights.

It wasn't until after my second pass at the jar that I even asked what I was drinking.

"My father would make this all the time," was the only explanation Piotr gave. "Though I've made my modifications." He told me that since by law there were no closed-circuit cameras allowed in the restrooms, he'd been able to hide the mixture in a series of toilet tanks over the last six months as we moved from floor to floor, and only this week had the concoction finally gotten to a place where he was satisfied with its potency.

The drink came back to me and I drank for a fourth time—I'd been sitting on the floor for what felt like an hour—my sips getting larger and more bold with each revolution. A pleasant electricity was passing through my body in slow, even waves. I knew what I was doing was wrong, for several reasons, but the feeling was undeniable. When the call for dinner came over the loudspeaker I had just finished another heavy swig, and standing up I had to brace myself on the lip of the sink to avoid falling over.

"Take this." Piotr offered me a stick of gum, a way of protecting his stash should the smell be discovered on my breath. Little did he know that I was a professional at hiding my drinking; that it was a skill I'd honed for many years.

Still, I accepted the gum for fear of how he might react should I have said no.

Delightfully drunk, I walked to the mess, my feet heavy, boots pendulous. I pulled boxed lasagna from a stack steaming on the counter and a Coke from the communal cooler and found a seat next to Saeed.

"How's your wife?" I asked, my fork full with flavorless noodles and rubbery cheese.

"What are you talking about?" Saeed cocked his head at me, his face twisted up like he had just smelled something terrible.

"Weren't we just—I mean, I thought..." I stuffed a load of noodles in my mouth to keep myself from talking further.

What was I doing? I waited for Saeed to respond, to say anything in order to guide us back into friendly territory, but instead he began to scroll through his phone, double-tapping on every other image. Perhaps he could sense it, my having been drinking. I don't think I was signaling it, but then the body infrequently knows what it's doing when not in control of its own facilities. I took stock of myself, did some shaky math. How many gulps had I taken? Just two? No, more. A lot more. Maybe. I wasn't sure and before long I noticed my dinner plate was empty and Saeed was standing up to bus his tray, leaving me with a curt goodbye.

I attempted to follow but was forced to sit back down, my balance faltering and the half-full Coke resting on my tray falling and spilling on the floor. I grabbed a wad of napkins and mopped it up as best I could, my hands and knees pressed into the hard linoleum. Beneath my palms it felt as though the ground was shaking. No, not shaking; thrumming, a low, steady rhythm. It wasn't uncommon for The Pinnacle to shudder when one of the many cranes was being erected on the topmost floor, but this was different. A warmth moved up my arms, into my chest, filling the spaces between my ribs and the parts of my body that allowed me to function. I found myself unable to pull my hands from the floor, as if they were stapled to it. The frequency of the rumbling sensation pulsed through my body in steady bursts until I found the pattern of my breathing synced alongside it. It's like I was praying to The Pinnacle, my body supplicated, the three-hundred floors beneath a vessel for my misplaced faith.

And then, nothing.

My fingers sticky from spilled Coke, I pulled my hands from the floor. I stood, this time more slowly, to find that the mess was mostly empty, all the men having returned to the rec room to watch television or take turns at the ping pong table. Henry was passed out on a plastic bench near the coat hooks. A small puddle of drool had accumulated on the ground beneath him.

I dropped my entire lunch tray into the garbage by mistake, but rather than fish it out I left it in the trash bin. My father, were he here, would have chided me. But he wasn't here.

I turned to see Piotr lingering at the entryway. He motioned to me and then cocked his head toward the restroom. I didn't want to sit for fear of passing out and knew Saeed wouldn't talk to me, so I followed Piotr into the bathroom. One of the general laborers was washing his face at the sink, and upon seeing us enter quickly left, the water still running.

"You can really handle it, can't you?" Piotr said.

We'd taken up residence in the handicap stall and

passed the jar, our knees touching in the cramped space. I belched and the sound echoed off the wall tiles.

"I suppose so."

"Yeah, you've been around. I can tell." He took a deep drink and handed me the jar. I'd lost track of how many times it had gone between us, but its contents were noticeably lighter than when we started. The liquid no longer tasted like anything, simply a warm sensation en route to my guts. I briefly imagined the hangover that awaited me, how much worse it would be in the din of the jobsite but washed the thoughts away with another sip of Piotr's homebrew. That was a problem for a different version of myself, one that, at that very moment, existed a very long distance away.

"You married?" Piotr asked.

We'd been silent for a long time, the only sounds being men coming in to piss and the atomic whir of the heated hand dryers that followed. If anyone saw us they didn't say anything, content to leave trouble alone.

"No," I responded, wiping some booze that had dribbled down my chin. "We live together, but we're not married." Usually I lied and said Embry was my wife, which was less complicated than explaining to people that she refused to marry me until I achieved an entire year of sobriety.

"What about you?" I asked.

"Was, once. But now with my schedule it's unlikely it'll ever happen again."

"It's hard to make it work, being home so infrequently."

"Yeah, or never."

What he told me next felt made up, like a folktale.

Before joining up with Robison-Moon, Piotr had been homeless, having gambled all of his money away on European football and being forcibly evicted when that was still legal. He'd gone from couch to couch until running out of friends and then found himself in the shelter system. He would work odd jobs here and there, pouring concrete or demolition, but any money made from that went to a combination of alimony and various chemical fixes: cigarettes, alcohol, crystal meth that he bought in Chinatown. When he saw that Robison-Moon was hiring and that they would also be providing accommodations he wasted no time in signing up. The company, in a rush to start construction, was uninterested in performing any kind of background check, or even conducting a formal interview for that matter, and he broke ground on day one. He was one of the few men who had worked on The Pinnacle for its entire construction. Still, he found that his paycheck was gone in only a few days after having cashed it, the funds drawn back into his vices.

"It was no life," he told me. "You see this here?" He pulled down the collar of his shirt and pointed to a patch of black, scaly skin the size of a half-dollar beneath his collar bone. "A guy I was buying crystal from burned me with a live wire because he thought I was a cop. I passed out and woke up in the alley behind a counterfeit purse sweatshop, left for dead. Someone had taken my shoes and rats had bitten nearly through one of my toes."

He found he was happiest, or at least most stable and thus, most likely to survive, when he was holed up in The Pinnacle, locked away from the outside. So, he proposed to the site manager that he would forgo his off week and work back-to-back shifts on the site. In essence, he would never leave, and since the developers were hungry to recoup their investment as quickly as possible, they allowed him to stay, to milk from him all of the energy they possibly could to help erect the building. He signed no additional or amended contract to avoid labor laws and was paid for his extra time through a discreet, unreported wire transfer directly to his bank. They even gave him a closet that only he had access to where he could store his possessions, of which he had few at that point.

Since then he had lived in The Pinnacle's barracks, having not stood on the ground, the true ground, in over a year. On hearing this I realized that I'd never seen him on the elevators before. He always seemed to simply appear at the jobsite. He was pale, ghoulishly so, from not having seen the sun since moving in. He'd seen the outside world only through Zone and television.

"What do you do with your paycheck?" I asked.

"It's all in an account somewhere. I could probably retire."

If The Pinnacle was truly to keep growing, the possibility existed that Piotr would die in the barracks of old age, locked inside the world's tallest building for much of his adult life. Though perhaps that was what he wanted.

Without realizing it I finished off the last of the booze, tipping the jar to my lips and finding it empty.

"Oh shit, sorry."

"I've got more." He took the jar from my hands and placed it delicately into the toilet tank behind him.

The light above us flickered on and off, signaling that it was time for bed. At a certain hour the lights would turn off completely, all of the other electronics—the phones, the pinball machine, even the coffee maker—would cease to work. This was Robison-Moon's way of keeping us from staying awake until odd hours, our next-day tiredness the root cause of so many workplace accidents. Not that they cared about our safety. Rather, if someone was, say, crushed by a pallet of drywall mud, there could be a stoppage in work, in money made.

Thirty minutes passed. The world was becoming exceptionally tilted, and I stood to make my way to bed, careful to balance myself against the stall door. I navigated to a urinal and relieved myself and when I turned around, I was face to chin with Piotr.

"I'm going to show you something," he said.

Against my better judgment, and perhaps partially in thanks for the gift of his alcohol, I said, "Yeah, sure," and before I could zip my fly back up he was guiding me out of the restroom and into the barracks, toward what I had no idea.

The barracks were dark save for the intermittent blinking of LEDs attached to charging smartphones. I allowed Piotr to lead me through the rec room and toward the elevator doors like an owner being pulled by their excitable dog.

Piotr stopped at the keypad which controlled the elevator and lifted the protective cover over the touchscreen. The illuminated panel threw shadows over his face which further dug out his many wrinkles. He could have been anywhere from forty to seventy years old.

"What are you doing?" I was talking louder than I should have, but it didn't matter. The sleep that we entered after a full workday was that of the dead, dreamless and steady, too tired even to snore. The barracks resembled a morgue, bodies beneath sheets and silence.

"If you fuck with that they'll fire you," I said.

"They aren't watching."

"What are you talking about? They're always watching." I gazed up at one of the cameras in a darkened corner and as I did the air conditioner kicked on as though it was aware of my noticing.

"In order to conserve power, they turn most of the electrics off when the shifts change over. That includes the audio and visual monitoring on whatever floor is currently sleeping. Anything to save money." The elevator doors slid open, and a rectangle of light sliced through the barracks. I could now make out Henry's passed-out body on the bench. He had pulled down a few heavy coats to use as a blanket and his shoes were in a pile on the floor.

"How did you know the code?"

"They haven't changed it once since the project

started. They used to tell us, back when the project was new, when there was less to explore and get lost in. I guess they forget about that." Piotr stepped into the elevator car and motioned that I join him.

"I don't know, should we be doing this?" I wasn't sure why Piotr was so interested that I accompanied him, or what, if anything, he had to show me. Though to say I wasn't curious about what went on in the rest of The Pinnacle would have been a lie. We all gossiped and spread rumors about squatters on the lower floors, of secret government testing grounds in the underground levels, colonies of feral rats the size of house cats dominating the boiler.

"It's fine, trust me."

Maybe it would be. Or maybe I was truly drunk for the first time in over three months and thirsting for the first opportunity for stupidity. I'd already indulged in one vice that night, what was another, and another?

I patted my pants pockets, making sure I had my phone—for what reason I was unsure—and stepped over the threshold into the idling elevator car. I'd never been inside the elevator when it wasn't crammed with people. It was large enough, by my estimation, to fit at least three grand pianos, maybe a fourth if you tilted it slightly. The doors closed behind me and the car began to move. No, it wasn't moving. The floor numbers weren't changing. I was simply drunk, the entire planet shifting around my spinning vision.

"I think something's going on," Piotr said.

"Yeah, I'm soused off my ass."

"There's no other crew on right now."

As opposed to the bathroom, the elevator car was quiet and without echo, the walls covered in thick sheets of padded foam to protect whatever cargo it hauled up or down. A row of fluorescent lights patterned the ceiling, their drone amplified like a swarm of insects.

"What are you talking about?" I replied. "Who's working the other shift?"

"No one. Both of the other teams that were supposed to finish out this week are gone."

"Both? What are you still doing here then?" I wondered why we weren't moving, and I sat on the floor as a wave of nausea rippled through me.

"I need to know you're not gonna freak out."

I told him that I wouldn't, though in truth I had no idea.

"I was working, right? Helping to hang ceiling tiles, and I fall off the ladder, hit my head on a bag of concrete. So they sent me down a few floors for a concussion assessment. They shine the light in my eyes, ask me to count down from one hundred by sevens. I'm fine, but the whole thing takes an hour. I get escorted back up to the jobsite by one of the site managers and when the doors open up onto the floor everyone is gone."

"We were told they left."

"More like vanished. Tool belts, hard hats, work gloves—all of it was still in the places I remember everyone working before I had gone, but now just laying on the floor, bodies absent. It was as though the whole crew, every single one, disintegrated. I didn't get to look for long. The site manager on the other team ushered me back into the elevator and I was taken to the empty barracks and made to sign an NDA. 'For what?' I asked, but they only responded with 'It's proprietary, simply routine.' Then they told me I had the rest of the day off. It wasn't long until you and your team showed up, but before that I was totally alone in the barracks, perhaps one of only a few people in the entire Pinnacle. I haven't seen any of the other crew since. They just disappeared."

I was drunk. We were drunk. I was somewhere I shouldn't have been, talking about something I shouldn't have been talking about. Piotr had hit his head, perhaps not for the first time.

But then, as so often happens, a blade of doubt ran through me. If what Piotr was telling me was true, then I was, in a sense, brought in as fodder, as well as the other men, people who, at any moment, could suffer a similar fate. How long until I, too, disappeared? I suddenly felt so incredibly tired, the effort to lift my head, to tilt it from side to side taking a monumental effort. I closed my eyes for a moment and had difficulty opening them back up.

"Do you understand?" He crossed over to the floor panel, not waiting for my answer before selecting a number. Sitting there, I could see how much larger Piotr was, how strong he seemed. I still didn't know what he wanted me to see so badly, but I was already so far along into whatever was going on that I felt compelled to say yes. I nodded, and then, as though I had incited the action, the elevator lurched into motion.

It seemed to be moving more slowly than it had even earlier that evening, as if it were heavily weighted. I threw up a bit into my mouth and rediscovered the taste of Piotr's homemade booze, though this time it burned not from the alcohol but my own internal acid.

"What about their families? How would they explain their loved ones just ceasing to exist?"

"Technically the company doesn't have to, not yet. There's still a few days until that crew is expected anywhere. Plus, I went down to the other barracks, and it was as if no one had ever been there. The cots and couches were covered with sheets of plastic, and everything smelled like disinfectant."

Did I know any of the people who had worked the shift before we arrived? I didn't believe so, not outside of Zone, anyway. We were all so sealed off from one another that we could have worked alongside a race of intelligent aliens and been unaware.

But I was a pragmatist, something I'd inherited from

my father, sure that whatever had taken place a few days before could be easily explained. To reach this explanation I decided to further humor Piotr—indulging him for sharing his liquor with me—and after I'd seen whatever mundane molehill he was mountain-making I would return to my bed and pass into a dreamless sleep.

A rush of air blew against my back as the elevator doors opened behind me, and turning around I could see the jobsite, though now totally unfamiliar. Ductwork hung unmoored from the ceiling, sheets of vinyl had been laid haphazardly over stacked paint cans, and everything was caked in a light layer of industrial dust. It wasn't how we had left it only a few hours earlier, the space was now totally trashed. Low light spilled in over the floor, like the kind that exists in the aftermath of a power outage, and from somewhere a draft pushed wisps of fiberglass insulation across the polished concrete. The entire area seemed somehow transformed. Nothing would stay still, my eyes seemingly rotating in my head, my steps unbalanced.

Piotr, his face now a slate of seriousness, motioned for me to step off the elevator and onto the site.

"What am I looking for?" I asked, placing one foot cautiously onto the work floor as though it were made of thin ice.

"Whatever the company didn't want us to see earlier. Whatever those guards were here to keep us away from."

"Wait, I didn't think—"

I had only enough time to pull back my other leg before the elevator closed sharply—operating by seemingly random motions—bifurcating the space between Piotr and myself. The suddenness of it put me back hard on my ass, and I found myself unable to sit up, hobbled by a strong urge to vomit. I could hear the elevator moving quickly down the shaft. I hadn't seen the code Piotr entered in to summon the elevator, and I had no idea if it was coming back. Perhaps he had gotten me drunk only to strand me up here, but for what purpose I wasn't sure. If anyone from Robison-Moon discovered me I would surely be fired, an outcome which seemed more and more likely as I accepted that Piotr had abandoned me.

Well past the euphoric phase of having consumed so much liquor, I found it more and more difficult to keep my eyes open, and as I stared into the unfinished ceiling I felt time pass slowly, my heart rate resting and then, like it had been the plan all along, I fell asleep at the top of the world.

YOUR *father wants pajamas,* is all my mother's text said.

What, like, for his birthday? I was waiting for Embry outside The Fat Chef, a diner she waitressed at back while she was still in school. When her shift got out, we were supposed to make an appearance at the engagement party of one of her friends. We had a car back then, a little Ford that had been long out of date even when it was new to us. To give it traction on the winter roads we'd weighed down the trunk with cement board cut-offs I'd taken from the dumpster at the jobsite I was working on at the time. I would total that car only a few months later driving it home from The Get Set, a bar near the airport. I suppose I shouldn't have been driving at all, a fact evidenced by the concrete abutment that I soon rammed into after taking a turn too wide. For fear of having my license suspended, I limped the car home and into the driveway where Embry discovered it the next morning. We sold it for scrap and got thirty-five dollars.

We're at the hospital. He wants the red pair, the cotton set.

The parking lot was suffused with the smell of sizzling bacon fat and every so often I caught glimpses of rats scurrying between dumpsters. Embry preferred I wait for her outside, even in the cold when the weather froze my nose hairs together. I guess she worried I'd do something stupid, embarrass her in some way, which was probable.

What do you mean, at the hospital?

I'd had a few beers before driving over, but I was fine behind the wheel. I felt pretty good, actually, warm despite the crusting of snow that had recently patterned the ground, full with high spirit in the face of having to withstand another one of Embry's friends' awful get-togethers, which always devolved into everyone becoming lost in their phones while leaning against various pieces of furniture.

Your father had his bypass today. We're at Medical Center Southeast.

On the adjacent street, a pair of small sedans spun their tires fruitlessly on the incline in front of a stoplight, languidly sliding back down the hill toward the Qwik Stop. This wasn't an uncommon occurrence, and thus no one felt obliged to go out of their way to help. It was understood that it was the driver's responsibility to right themselves, to become educated on what to do. Often cars came to a stop naturally, before any damage could be done. Then they either tried again to scale the hill—which usually resulted in the same Sisyphean loop—or rerouted toward one of the larger streets freshly plowed and coated with road salt. Though of course there were rare times when a car unequipped to handle the conditions would surmount the slope, though not without great difficulty, and continue on their way to Bon Vivant Fine Liquors or The Reptile Hut or Mattress Warehouse USA. It was quite a thing to witness.

What bypass? Did something happen?

I wondered if perhaps I was reading the texts wrong. My mother seemed so calm, as though nothing was wrong. If I understood her correctly then my father had undergone major surgery, a thought which, even in my inebriated state, landed heavy in my gut. It wasn't out of character for my parents to withhold things from me, especially when it pertained to their own mortality, but this felt different somehow. My father could have died so easily. In thinking this I attempted to remember the last thing I said to him, how meaningful it might have been. Though it was probably some mundane something not worth committing to memory.

Assholes.

I reminded myself to be empathetic. They had gone through something terrible, and hadn't I been spared the stress? But hadn't my existence in the important moments of their life been erased in some way also? I attempted to puzzle out all the possible intentions they could have had for not telling me but soon stopped. Or perhaps they had just forgotten to tell me? It wasn't worth worrying over. He was alive, clearly, my father. I suppose that was what mattered.

Through the windows the restaurant looked a bit like an old oil painting, the weathered glass distorting and blurring the shapes which moved behind it. I could just make out Embry as she let down her hair and pulled on the pair of mittens I'd gotten her last Christmas. There was something foil-wrapped in her hands, and she passed it from palm to palm to avoid prolonged exposure to its heat.

No. This was scheduled.

When?

For two months now.

As Embry pushed through the restaurant door, a wave of humid, greasy air plumed out into the cold.

"You ready?" she asked, sliding into the passenger seat.

"Yeah, but we need to make a stop first. My dad's in the hospital."

"Is he okay?"

"I think so? I don't know." I told her all I knew. I plugged my phone into the center console, an aftermarket addition installed by one of Embry's friends. Through it my mother's texts came to me via the speakers in an even, digitized voice slightly tinted with an English accent.

He says they're in the dryer.

"So they just weren't going to tell you?" Embry had unwrapped the foil and passed me a mozzarella stick which I held between my fingers like a cigarette as I drove.

"I don't know what they were going to do. Maybe they didn't want to worry me."

Also, can you bring me one of those iced coffees from the fridge? The dairy-free kind.

"Bypass, that's open-heart right?" Embry asked.

"I think so."

Maybe a toothbrush, too? Yeah, me and your father's.
Please.
Thank you.
Love you.

We were silent all the way to my parent's house, the sound of the car muffled by the snow-lined backstreets. When I pulled into the driveway there was a small rectangle of cleared asphalt where my father's truck had been parked that morning.

"I mean, they would have called you if something bad happened."

"Mhmm," I replied. "Probably."

My mother curtailed my father's hoarding and obsessive tinkering in the years since I moved out. The house was, consequently, relatively clean. The horizontal surfaces that had before been piled upon with junk—the sideboard, the dining room table, the kitchen counters—were clear. The only sign of any disturbance was a coat rack that had been recently knocked over by the startled cat.

Forgive the mess.

Embry went to go find the thermostat while I made

my way downstairs to the laundry room, feeling along the walls in the dark. The single bulb flung shadows through the basement, swinging by its cord from the unfinished ceiling. I could hear Embry moving about the house, the floorboards letting out small, desultory moans, a noise which was soon replaced by the hum of the furnace stirring to life. I fished my father's pajamas from the dryer and folded them neatly. The fabric, a dark red plaid, was heavily pilled and smelled strongly of lint, as though it had been sitting for many days beneath a week's worth of laundry. I could recall this exact pajama set from when I was a child; seeing it on Christmas morning or on weekdays when I had early classes at school. My father was the type to retain, to keep that which he preferred and held dear. The frames of his glasses were the same since his early twenties, same with the brush he used to clean his shoes, the bristles now plastic stumps, items in the last moments of their usefulness. Whether intentional or not, I've taken on some of this same habit, finding myself in possession of things that any rational person would have thrown out years ago: broken smartphones, boxes filled with old wristwatches, airline tickets from the last five years in a rubber-banded stack.

Adjacent to the laundry room was a space I seldom entered while growing up. It was a large closet cramped with my father's rarely used tools and boxes of clothes addressed but not yet sent—they never would be, I realized—to the First Methodist Church clothing drive. My brother told me that someone had been murdered in the room, that our house was once the site of a bloodied and viscera-splattered crime scene, an idea which terrified me. I later learned that he said this so that he could hide things in there without my knowing, mainly weed he didn't want to share and a little bit of ecstasy that his friends had scored at a college party.

"You find them?" Embry called out from the top of the stairs.

I told her that I did and that I would be up in a minute.

I set my father's pajamas on top of the dryer and stepped in front of the closet door. The knob, plain aluminum colored to look like brass, was worn in the grooves where a palm would rest. I allowed my hand to lay upon it and it began to turn slowly, as though it were moving on its own, but of course it wasn't; it was me.

A wooden workbench, the same one that had been in the garage while I was growing up, occupied the room now, and atop it were boxes of my father's old inventions. The entire space, in fact, was stacked floor to ceiling with stuff, so much so that I had to turn sideways to move, sidling beside towers of what most people would rightly call garbage. Out of curiosity, I pulled a box from a nearby stack and poured its contents out onto the workbench top.

I remembered this.

Somehow my father had gotten ahold of five feet of aluminum pipe—perhaps he had purchased it from the hardware store, but more likely he found it in someone's trash. Using his crude knowledge of welding he had bonded several of the tubes together and sealed one end. Then, using the chain from my bicycle—which he took without telling me, an action which I only realized when I was already embarrassingly late for my summer job as a hotel valet the next day—fashioned a set of gears that, when enmeshed, spun the series of tubes around and around. He had created, in essence, a minigun, one that he filled with Roman candles and presented to my brother and I on the Fourth of July. For the entire evening the three of us—my mother stayed on the porch—sprayed sparks at one another, spiraling a cocktail of chemicals at our improvised shields of garbage can lids. As far as his inventions went, it was pretty successful.

I set the contraption down and retrieved another box. Among a tangle of pillaged electrical wires, a half-empty bottle of cheap Hungarian vodka lay hidden, no doubt carefully placed there by my father. I grabbed the bottle and, as though it were an automatic gesture, unscrewed the cap, taking a deep pull from the neck before returning it as best I could so as to appear undisturbed. I didn't expect him to confront me about it when he got home and discovered some had gone missing. That would require an admission on both our parts. I hoisted the box back onto its stack and lifted the aluminum tubing again, its weight satisfying in the cradle of my hand.

"You alright?"

I turned to face Embry, the minigun pointed directly at her.

"Jesus," she jumped back a bit. "What the hell is that thing?"

"Just one of many pieces that comprise my father's legacy." I gestured around the space. With the boxes stacked so high, little light could get through, and it felt as though we were deep underground. Embry had never seen any of my father's creations. Though she'd heard stories, especially from him, of their grandeur. To hear my father tell it he was simply waiting for the inevitable call from the Nobel committee.

"You are your father's legacy," Embry said, taking the contraption from my hands and placing it on the workbench. "And the best part of it, as far as I'm concerned." She kissed me on the cheek. Her breath smelled like fried food. "Christ, there's so much of it."

"Yeah, pretty much every creative idea he's had in his entire adult life is in this room."

"I guess."

"What?"

"I'm just upset. He should have told you. What if he had died?"

I've wondered a lot if my father was meant to be a parent. I have no doubts that he is a good person, but I can't convince myself he was a good dad. He gave himself value based on his ability to interact and change that which he saw could be made better, more efficient in his eyes. But people aren't like that. They make their own moves, carve out their own lives. I realized then that, if he had died it would have been more like losing a dear friend than losing a parent.

Embry and I were silent long enough for the furnace to cycle off, and it wasn't until I was by his side in the hospital, watching him sleep through the remnants of the surgical anesthetic, that I recalled leaving the closet door open. When he returned home, he would know I had trespassed. He would know what I knew. No one can hide forever.

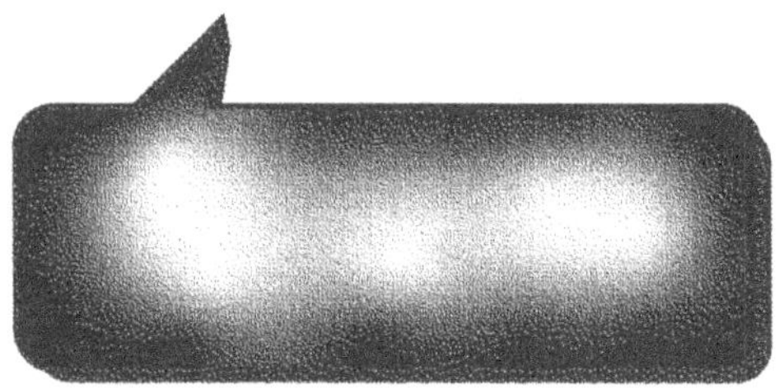

A cool wind blew across my face. I could tell it was wind and not exhaust from one of the many open vents on the jobsite. Wind has a quality to it, something natural. I'd never felt it while working on The Pinnacle, sealed away as we were.

I was still on the floor, my back aching from the concrete, and a series of red lights, like those in a photographer's dark room, shone along the walls, casting blood-tinted shadows. Across the floor, near where, had the space not been enclosed by heavy plastic, there would have been floor-to-ceiling windows overlooking the southern half of Manhattan all the way to Staten Island, there was an intense flapping sound. I pushed myself up, still unsteady but able to at least stand still. There was a large, diagonal tear in the sheeting that covered where the glass would soon be installed. The cut was clean, as if made by a surgeon's scalpel, and while it looked small from a distance, I moved closer and saw that I could easily step through it and out into the open air. The material that surrounded the in-progress floors of The Pinnacle was, to my knowledge, virtually indestructible, so whatever had torn through it must have been intensely strong and moving at a horrifying speed.

I'd never seen the city from so high up. Remarkably,

there were no low clouds, no fog, and beneath me the spires from smaller buildings—still massive if viewed from the ground—twinkled like distant stars. Birds, their figures so slight as to be nearly invisible, winged far below. The air that passed through the tear was a different air than what flowed down on the ground. It was sweeter, somehow purer, untainted by exhaust and urine-scented steam. I recalled that my phone was in my pocket and, seeing a portal to the outside, something away from Robison-Moon's all-seeing eye, pulled it out to check if I had reception. Embry's face stared back at me from the lock screen, a party streamer in her mouth and two middle fingers held high. As I extended my arm out through the torn plastic the reception bars gradually increased. If I could call Embry, she could get in touch with someone at Robison-Moon, or Saeed, or even the fire department, as though I were a cat up a tree in need of saving, and they could come and fetch me. I'd still be fired, but at least I would be spared the shame of being discovered by my team the next morning huddled on the ground shivering beneath a makeshift blanket cobbled together from carpet swatches. I reached out a bit more, supporting myself on a piece of unpainted sheetrock. My head and shoulders were now entirely outside The Pinnacle.

If I fell it would be an entire minute before I turned to bodily sludge on the sidewalk, plenty of time to think about all the stupid choices that had led up to that moment. My life would cease to be anything but a math problem: at what point does a worthless drunk reach terminal velocity? But I was far from sober and desperate not to spend an entire night up on the jobsite floor.

I brought Embry up in my contacts. I could see but not hear city buses lurching from stop to stop. Lights flicked on in nearby high-rises, their glow diffused by curtains. The large lighted displays in Times Square—which had grown considerably taller over the last few years—

were familiar to me from my trips to the jobsite: Broadway shows, CBD patches, a new phone app where users could send one another anonymous flirty questions. A private plane was on its way into JFK, and I looked down on it as it made its way over the river. It felt like I was flying.

"Hello?" Embry, unprepared to receive a video call, struggled to find the switch for the bedside lamp.

"Baby, I need you to do something for me. Are you listening?"

"Is everything okay?" The pixels that constituted her shadow evaporated as the screen filled with light. She took out her mouthguard and placed it on the headboard. "What time is it?"

"I need you to call the number on the fridge." I was yelling over the wind, which seemed to whip my words away as they left my mouth.

"Okay, sure, sure. Wait, huh? What's going—"

There was a nudge and then another, and then a push at my legs that sent my whole upper body out through the tear.

My throat was a fist, and for a moment I pictured the end of my life, imagined seeing all of the completed floors of The Pinnacle pass quickly before me, my reflection projected onto each as individual frames in a tragic movie. Embry's face fell away, my phone tumbling over and downwards until I could no longer see her. I was just barely hanging on to the plastic with one hand while the other flailed for something sturdier. I vomited and the stream of my puke blew back against the side of the building, plastering itself against the window.

Using the hand supporting me from inside the building, I pulled myself back through the tear and fell onto my hip, the spirit fully knocked from my chest. I pressed a hand into one of my back pockets, checking for fear that I had soiled myself. But instead, my hand found something else, and I turned over to discover Ponshu idling behind me, its red connectivity LED flashing on and off like a blinking eye.

"No fucking way," I said, pushing it away and turning onto my side.

Again, Ponshu prodded at me, rolling back and nosing my spine with its front bumper like an impatient child. I'd never been on the jobsite during my off hours, but I assumed that the measuring robots were deactivated when not in use. To see Ponshu now, animated in a way that made it seem almost alive, felt surreal.

I got to my feet and, in a moment of undirected rage, punted Ponshu across the room, where it landed against a pile of stacked aluminum track. Because I still had my steel-toes on, this was relatively painless. From there, Ponshu righted itself and began to move toward the plywood barricade that ran through the center of the floor. The guards from before were gone, and the spaces upon which they stood were now occupied only by two sets of boot prints outlined by drywall dust. There was a small opening in the barrier, and Ponshu struggled to squeeze through, plastic bits dislodged by my kick rattling inside its body. The thought of having lashed out and hurt it made me a bit sad, and could it understand me, I would have told it I was sorry. I suddenly wanted to make sure it was okay, and I walked toward the opening in the barrier it had disappeared through in search of it.

I had my theories about why the plywood was there. My first thought was that there had been a terrible accident, that someone from the previous team had been maimed, their shredded body and the bloodstained floor hidden from us to curtail gossip. There was also the possibility that Robison-Moon was participating in something illegal, and that the partition was there simply to hide the activity. There were many who believed that The Pinnacle was erected simply as a never-ending way to launder money. The most plausible of my theories, however, was that the company was, as they had many times before, simply withholding some piece of information from the workers for fear that if it was known we would consider selling these industry secrets to other interested parties in China or Brazil or Russia.

And perhaps because I was going to be fired anyway, I followed Ponshu behind the barricade, forcing a wide enough opening between the boards so that I could just barely slip through. What, after all, did I have to lose? Perhaps I would stumble onto something and Robison-Moon would pay for my silence. These were drunken aspirations, of course, a sort of optimism fueled by a combination of the alcohol's lingering effects and a need to find a silver lining to a situation I had no idea how I would communicate to Embry.

Oh God, Embry. The process of explaining myself unscrolled before me: the lies I would have to concoct, the long series of half-truths. Maybe I wouldn't lie. Maybe I would tell her that I had gotten drunk, exceptionally drunk, at work in the shared bathroom and then followed someone I barely knew up into a restricted area and then passed out before dropping my phone an entire mile down onto the pavement. I would tell her that our income would decline in the wake of my inevitable termination, that we may need to move in with her parents. Maybe I wouldn't stop there. Maybe I would tell her that I never really quit drinking, that I had bottles hidden everywhere, that out back in the container where I kept the deicing salt there was buried an entire case of beer. Maybe I would tell her that, on the night she stayed with my father at the hospital so that I could go home and rest, I instead went to Canteen and drank myself stupid. Maybe I would tell her that every single promise I'd made about my sobriety had been a falsehood, that I never wanted to be sober at all, and that at times I wanted to drink more than I wanted to live, a paradox that fueled binge after binge after binge. Many times I imagined a conversation taking place between us in which she asked me what it would take to get me to stop drinking. The answer, I realized, but only in this fictional dialogue, was that I didn't want to stop, that I would be content to keep drinking until I died. That of course meant losing her, and in effect losing myself. I wasn't okay with that, but I couldn't convince my brain that the two halves—Embry, whom I loved, and alcohol, which I also loved—sat on discrete sides of the same scale, and that choosing one meant sending the other to the hard ground.

I knew what I was doing. I was in control. Yet there was nothing I could do to stop myself. It would go on and on and on, my hand held over the open flame.

A glow coming from behind the plywood—had it always been there or had I just now noticed?—changed gradually from peach to orange to yellow, the light shining in a halo through the jamb of the iron door that sat just beyond. A sign pasted to it read "NO ENTRY" in six different languages. I couldn't see Ponshu anywhere, which was odd given that the space behind the plywood was only as large as the interior of a normal elevator car, barely enough room to fully extend one's arms.

I thought about Saeed and the others asleep in the barracks, the people filing out of bars at the onset of last call, the subway engineers barreling through the city with a barely-full train of cars, the demolition crews blasting through rock in order to make way for gigabit internet cable, the layers and layers of schist laced through with fossils that run beneath the island of Manhattan, the hard mantle, the strata of molten rock, and then, finally, a liquid core so unfathomably hot that it bears no comparison to anything else, a swirling, amorphous ball of fire that will one day be entirely swallowed up by another, much larger ball of fire, extinguishing all that has ever existed and, if we have not found our way to other worlds, the written record of humanity—the tokens of my father, my mother, my brother, Embry—save for those lucky satellites launched far away into unknown space, hurtling toward a society that will examine the etchings and wonder about a civilization beyond their own stars.

I placed both palms on the door and pushed my way inside.

I knew The Spike only by the tiny redacted circle that represented it on the floor plans we had each been given, small enough in comparison to the rest of The Pinnacle that it could easily be obscured by the tip of a finger. The Spike was the thing about the building that most interested journalists, as its precise function and construction was a closely guarded secret, one which was to be kept within "the Robison-Moon family." The Ukrainians flown in to construct it were similarly secretive. Science writers from *The New York Times* and scores of tech bloggers had attempted to find out as much as they could about The Spike, some even breaking into the building and promptly being escorted—often without their cameras and notepads—to a waiting NYPD patrol car.

I wasn't a structural engineer, so I could only guess at the validity of the claims Robison-Moon made about it, that it somehow—and on this they would not elaborate—ensured that the building would not collapse during or after its construction in the event of something like an earthquake or, as if it were totally normal, a jet strike.

The room I found myself inside was a cylinder ringed by a narrow metal catwalk, The Spike at its center. The space was smaller than I had imagined. Realistically you could take only one full step before you collided with the guardrail, beyond which was a deep shaft tapering to a faraway point. The Spike itself was not large—to circumnavigate the entire chamber took only ten steps. If I wrapped my arms around it, I would have had no problem clasping my hands together, perhaps even grabbing my wrists. As this was the top of the building (at the moment, anyway)

The Spike was rounded off on top, like the eraser on the end of a giant metal pencil.

And it was spinning.

The same yellow light that seeped through the plywood now emanated from The Spike itself, and as I stared, the color gradually changed to green, then purple, then back to yellow.

I shouldn't have been there. I knew this, and yet, as though something outside of my consciousness were controlling my body, I reached a hand out and let it rest on The Spike's smooth surface, its slow movement like water passing under my palm. I began to feel the same sensation I had experienced in the mess, my whole body drumming. I leaned forward, my hips a fulcrum resting on the guardrail. I could, if I wanted, place my forehead on The Spike and linger while it gradually ground my skin away, its motion no faster than the second hand on a wristwatch. I could kiss The Spike, taste it. I could point my face down into the glowing abyss and plummet until I discovered whatever it was that The Spike was barreling down into.

But I couldn't do any of these things, because I was no longer in the chamber with The Spike. I was no longer in The Pinnacle. I was no longer in New York City.

Instead, I was in my parents' kitchen, seated at the table while my father sat in one of the dining room chairs, his posture rigid and his face in profile. My mother had draped a black bed sheet behind him, upon which she taped a piece of white cardstock. The workshop lamp, which had for so long been attached to my father's workbench in the garage, was pointed at the side of his face, projecting his shadow onto the paper. My mother stood between my father and the sheet, adjusting his position, then began to trace the shadow with a carpenter's pencil. They continued like this, in silence—there wasn't even the ambient sound of evening coming in through the open kitchen window— until the silhouette was complete, a shadow version of my father cast onto the wall behind him as though an explosion had blasted away all but his outline. He stood and removed the paper, and while he and my mother discussed it and pointed at features that surprised them, their hair began to grow long, and they hunched over as though piled on greatly with stones. The wrinkles already present on their faces deepened and expanded, and then, no longer able to withstand the weight of their bodies, both of them sat and began to fold the piece of paper into smaller and smaller squares until the two of them disappeared completely, snuffed like a withering flame. I attempted to stand, but found myself instead transported once more, this time hovering over the bed Embry and I shared back in New Haven. I watched Embry shift in her sleep, the side of the bed I would normally have occupied empty. Embry's easel was set up in the opposite corner, and on it a canvas was stretched taut, bands of color running vertically down its surface and pooling on the floor. The paint accumulated at a rapid pace, as though flowing from the painting's surface like water from a mountain spring, and soon the room was flooded with paint, colors blending to make an inky black which gradually reached the top of our mattress. I knew there was nothing I could do, and Embry was soon swallowed up, her entire body disappearing beneath the liquid. Then, as the paint started to recede, she was gone, the bed vacant save for the impression of her body on the fitted sheet. The paint retreated back into the canvas quickly, and then I was falling, or at least I experienced the sensation of falling, the force of gravity rushing against my chest, my arms blown back behind me, though I stayed in place, levitating but dropping, floating and sinking. Without warning I collided with something invisible, and I pulled my hand away from The Spike and slotted it neatly into my pocket.

I left the chamber quickly, the lights from The Spike now shifting between coral and blue. I placed the plywood back as it had been before and stared out the tear in the plastic. It was still night, the wind from before having died away. Either no time had passed or very much. A quiet ding went off behind me and, like a doorway into bright sun, the elevator doors parted to reveal an empty car, the floor number of the barracks already punched in. I boarded and allowed it to take me down, an uneventful trip, after which I stepped out. Everyone was still asleep. I found my bed and fell into dreamless sleep immediately, reprieved.

EMBRY was appropriately sour on the phone the following morning.

"I spent hours, literally hours, trying to get in touch with someone from your work. I called the company, I called 311, and then the police. And do you know what they asked me? They asked, 'Does your husband,'—and here I had to correct them and inform them that you were not my husband—they asked, 'Does your husband drink?' And I could have lied and told them no, but I didn't want to begin whatever farce was about to take place by lying to the police, so I said, 'Occasionally.' And do you know how they responded? Do you? They told me that all the wives of alcoholics—and again, I pointed out to them that I was not your wife, that we were not married—said that their husbands only drank occasionally. They told me to wait for you to call in the morning, that you were probably somewhere sleeping it off and had forgotten to charge your phone. Then they hung up. And you know what? I believed them. Still, I wasn't able to get back to sleep, and I was just about to call a taxi to take me into the city to go looking for you when you called. I haven't slept, and right now I want to be relieved so badly to know that you're safe, but I can't get past these shards of anger that are shooting out from every part of my body."

The series of beeps notified me that I was near the end of my allotted time on the barrack phones.

"I lost my phone, hon, that's all."

"And were they right? Were you drinking?"

I told her I hadn't, a lie that was accompanied by a shiver through my body.

"How could I?" I asked. "How could I have gotten drunk in The Pinnacle?"

"If I don't hear from you tonight after your shift, if you don't explain all of this, then I won't be here when you get back. Okay?"

"I'll call, I promise. Right after I get out and am back in the barracks." I said these words but didn't mean them. Not because I wasn't intent on keeping my word and returning home to Embry, but rather because the entirety of my mental energy—depleted as it was with my exceptional hangover—was focused on recalling the events of the night before.

"Fine, just know that if you don't, then—"

The call cut out and an automated voice informed me that I had used up all of the minutes available to me for the next six hours. I replaced the receiver in its cradle and made my way slowly to the mess. I didn't know that I could eat—I didn't want to risk throwing up in the elevator, its dreaded motion—but I knew that I wanted to sit, to maybe have some coffee so that I seemed less sluggish on the jobsite. I passed Henry and he avoided my gaze like an embarrassed child. The bench that he slept on was still covered by his makeshift overcoat blanket. The smell of cardboard-carton orange juice turned my stomach as I made my way through the breakfast line. I grabbed a can of cold brew—the only coffee options available to us were various vending machine concoctions bottled in South Korea—and sat down beside Saeed, who uncharacteristically had his phone tucked away in his shirt pocket.

"Nothing good on Zone?"

"Nothing at all on Zone." He spooned instant oatmeal into his mouth.

"What do you mean?" I took a sip of coffee, and it dripped down into my empty stomach.

"Servers are down or something, I don't know. Can't even open the app, you just get an error message."

The rest of the team filtered in and out of the mess, completely oblivious to whatever was going on three floors above. Not that I had any better idea. I tried to replay the events of the previous night. The memories were clear: Piotr's confession, the elevator, hanging outside of The Pinnacle by my fingertips. While these events, this timeline, was true to me, years of blackout drinking had shown me that my memories and reality were incongruous. What I knew with certainty was what I experienced after touching The Spike. I saw my parents, saw Embry, witnessed each of them disappear. I could write down every second of those experiences on paper. But how could they have happened, and who would believe me? I had spoken just now to Embry, corporeal and cogent if not pissed off. I was no crackpot. I know what I felt, the visions laced firmly in my mind, their detail unlike that of a dream in their ease of recollection, of feeling. I went somewhere, of this I was sure. I turned these two truths in my mind, their ends repelled from one another like out-of-sequence magnets.

I looked around the mess for Piotr as some sort of confirmation, but he was nowhere to be found. I entertained, if only briefly, the idea that he never existed at all. Perhaps I was losing my mind. Perhaps it was already gone.

"You look terrible."

This was the meanest thing Saeed had ever said to me. I was almost too stunned to answer, though I remembered that I offended him last night somehow, so I let it slide through me. I considered telling him about the lack of surveillance, but in doing so I would have outed my trespassing. I trusted Saeed, but his ill-temper toward me, however justified, made me nervous that he would turn around and relay that same information to Noor. I decided to keep what I experienced to myself.

"I didn't sleep well."

"You were trashed."

"I wasn't."

"You smelled like nail polish remover. You still do." Saeed looked at me as if he knew what Piotr and I had done beyond simply drinking ourselves stupid. But he couldn't have known. Right?

I pushed myself away from the table and told him that I would see him on the floor, then went to the restroom and emptied my insides for what felt like hours. When I was finally done, I bathed in the shallow sink and went to retrieve my gear to head up with the rest of the team. I reached for my phone where it would normally be on the bed's built-in shelf before remembering that I lost it on the jobsite floor. I'd dropped it, right? I looked again for Piotr to ask him why he had left me up on the floor alone, but, again, he wasn't anywhere around. His bed was made neatly, his meager possessions—a small cast iron cross, two pairs of eyeglasses, a copy of a large book with an unreadable Polish title, and a framed photo of some unknown blonde woman—were arranged neatly on the bedside table. So he was real. I suppose that, knowing what I knew about him and his access to the building, he could have been anywhere, on any floor, even out on the street getting a bacon, egg, and cheese from a bodega.

Saeed gave me space on the elevator, avoiding eye contact as Noor called roll.

"Okay, let's go on then," she said.

"What about Piotr?" I asked. His name hadn't been called and the space he usually took up in the elevator, in the far back corner, was instead filled by another man.

"Mr. Nowak isn't feeling well. He's down in medical being examined. He won't be joining us today."

Saeed glared at me, and I met his gaze with a shrug of my shoulders, as if to say that I was as ignorant as he was as to what had happened. To an extent I was.

Piotr seemed fine last night, at least enough to convince someone else to accompany him on whatever journey he had established for the two of us. Whether or not he was truly sick I couldn't say, but I did find it odd that he was absent. As the elevator began to move, I recalled what he told me about the previous crew, that he'd been spared whatever fate had befallen them because he was somewhere else at the moment in question. Perhaps his absence was a kind of omen, and when the doors opened, we would all be disintegrated or shot or sucked into some vortex that stretched out our bodies until we no longer resembled human beings.

But no. Everything was familiar. Noor simply directed us to our work stations and laid out the plan for the day before letting us loose. The plastic sheet that tore the night before was mended as though nothing had happened. The floor was tidy and organized, things tucked away as to not hang down. Two armed guards framed the space where I had pushed the plywood aside the night before. Even Ponshu was roving around, humming from wall to wall and sending measurements down to the servers on the street. Though was there a hitch in its motion?

What if nothing at all interesting had happened? Perhaps Piotr and I had ridden the elevator, explored the vacant floor, and gone back to the barracks, content on having seen nothing of interest. The thought occurred to me that the fall I took leaving the elevator the night before had resulted in a concussion, and that everything I saw had been a wild hallucination. Though I wondered also if any of it mattered. I had gotten away with whatever occurred, at least on a professional level. What waited for me at home was another story.

Saeed and I worked the day side by side in silence,

communicating in head nods and gestures until our shift was over. I never did find my phone, sure then that it was now particulate dust in some West 31st Street gutter. Aside from that the shift passed entirely without incident, further plunging me into uncertainty, unable to trust my own hazy recollections.

"Your father is here," Embry said. I called her, as promised, as soon as we got back down to the barracks. I still had my vest and hard hat on.

"Like, at the house?"

"He just showed up. I guess he thought you'd still be here on account of it being your off week."

"What does he want?" I could hear someone in the background going through kitchen cupboards. Whenever my father visited he always set himself to little projects: a cabinet door that was loose on its hinges, a drawer whose slide needed oiling, floorboard nails poking up and catching on socks. Every time after he left, Embry and I would invariably find something misplaced, my father having moved it in his quest for optimization—measuring cups in a different spot, the Christmas tree stand relegated to the crawlspace—something which, when I asked him about it, he believed made the house "run more smoothly." Ask your mother, he had said. She can attest.

"To talk to you I suppose. I'll put him on."

I became aware of the time on the keypad; I had only two minutes left before I would be cut off until morning.

"Wait, before you do…" I paused. "Are we okay?" In asking this I was truly probing for some clarification about what had actually happened the night before, that her response would throw light onto my memory.

"Here he is."

I wasn't sure she heard me. Or perhaps she had and chose not to answer. Regardless, her voice on the phone was replaced by my father's.

"Where are you?" he asked.

This was often the way conversations between my father and I started. Not with a greeting, but with an interrogation.

"I'm at work, in the city."

"And you're sure?" He sounded frenzied, almost as though he was in the process of being physically restrained.

"Of course. What do you mean?"

"You're going to think I'm crazy."

I watched the seconds tick away on the keypad, worried that I wouldn't get to talk to Embry again before my father was finished speaking.

"I saw you last night," he said. "You were at the kitchen table and you were staring at the wall. I'd gone to get a glass of water and there you were. I tried to get your attention, calling your name and walking over to you, but you didn't respond. When I finally went to grab your shoulder, to shake you and ask what you were doing here, you disappeared. When I told your mother this she wondered if I hadn't dreamt it instead. Maybe I did, but it felt real in a way I can't quite articulate."

I was silent for a moment. If what he was saying was true, we had both been a part of the same experience, each of us witnessing something to which the other had no access.

"Are you there?" he asked.

"Yeah, I'm here."

"Don't you think that's bizarre?"

"Dad, I was drinking last night. I was drunk." There were only twenty seconds left on the call. Nineteen. Eighteen. "And, I don't know." Fifteen. "I was up on the floor," Nine, "and I feel like I saw something," Five, "or I went somewhere and—"

The series of beeps sounded and I responded by slamming the receiver back into its cradle. The words *please be gentle* scrolled by on the keypad display.

"Your woman giving you trouble?" Henry was at the

phone beside mine preparing to punch in a number.

"All due respect, Henry," I replied, "shut the fuck up."

Instead of eating dinner I went straight to bed, failing to find sleep through the sound of yelling over a game of Mexican Train. The lights were still on—we had no way of turning them off ourselves, just another way Robison-Moon held dominion over our time in The Pinnacle—so I buried my face beneath the pillow and watched as a nebulous parade of colors passed behind my closed eyelids.

Somehow my father and I experienced a similar vision. I was almost certain that I had not left The Pinnacle the night before—at least my body hadn't—and so explaining my appearance in his kitchen was difficult. It was just another in a series of questions that were taking up space in my mind. Piotr was still not with us, and I wondered if he would ever be back. Perhaps his knowledge of The Pinnacle's security had been discovered and he was fired. Though if that were the case, why did I still have a job? Wouldn't he have told them? Maybe he had more integrity than that, but he also didn't owe me anything. In assuming that he was gone I realized that I would never again have the opportunity to drink his homemade liquor; I had checked the bathrooms upon waking up and found only the empty jar.

I thought at that moment, perhaps more seriously than ever before, about quitting Robison-Moon. There were certainly other jobs I could get in New Haven, though the pay would be half of what I made working on The Pinnacle. I made a mental list of the perks that would accompany a new job: getting to sleep in my own bed every night, seeing the sun on a more consistent basis, eating what I wanted, when I wanted. But that freedom was in itself a certain kind of curse. In New Haven, I could drink. I knew where all the bars in the city were, which ones would serve me well past the limits of my own judgment. There would be very little to stop me from packing a beer in my lunchbox or going out with my coworkers after our shift ended. The Pinnacle was, in this way, a sort of monastery, and I was one of its many monks, temptation barred and with plenty of time for reflection. Though if I never quit, if I stayed on with Robison-Moon indefinitely, I would be stuck in a project with no end date, the tower itself rising and rising until the supports that held its untold weight in place sheared and the entire structure came crashing down, obliterating everything beneath. Entire generations could live and die, the length of their existence measured by how many floors The Pinnacle contained.

I fell asleep with the pillow over my face but woke up at some time during the night. I had been having inconsequential dreams, unintelligible parades of sensation that, upon waking, I couldn't recall. The lights had gone out some time ago and the beds around me were filled with sleeping bodies. I'd been jostled awake by a low rumbling that I could still feel. It was like being beside a busy freeway or walking along the track as a train passed. By the way in which everyone around me remained still I could sense that I was the only one experiencing the feeling, and I laid back down and pressed the pillow into my face again to try and muffle whatever was going on inside of my body.

I heard the familiar sound of the elevator doors opening, and, slowly, a line of light grew in the aisle between the two rows of beds, like a hidden path emerging in the beam of a full moon. I set my bare feet upon the cool linoleum and wrapped the blanket around my body like a shroud, intent on investigating whatever was going on with an unclouded mind. I stepped into the slice of light and the vibrations running through me became more intense to the point where it felt as though they might bring me to my knees, an inner earthquake. I walked toward the open elevator doors, the sterility of its empty insides, dragging the blanket behind me like a long wedding train. I was only wearing boxer shorts and an undershirt. Everything outside of the light fell into amorphous shadow. The rumbling increased as I approached the elevator, as though my body were a divining rod pointed toward plentiful water. I was being instructed. I was to board the elevator car and allow it to take me wherever it wanted. I pulled the edges of the blanket tighter around me and stepped over the gap onto stamped metal. I considered for a moment whether or not I was still dreaming. I bit the inside of my cheek and tasted the iron of blood on my tongue.

A shape approached through the light from the open doors. Its edges grew more and more defined and soon it was standing at the threshold, holding the doors open with the flat of its palm.

"What are you doing?" Saeed was wearing a tattered Mets t-shirt and gym shorts. His hair, which he slicked back every day, was spread messily across his forehead. "Get out of there, you could get fired for this!" The doors attempted to close but, as if on instinct, he reversed them with his hand, a gesture we were both startled by. Perhaps the doors weren't as strong as we were led to believe, but I suppose that wouldn't be so surprising, given what Piotr had told me about Robison-Moon's penchant for hyperbole. "I knew something was up, you'd been acting so strange. So what, you're just sneaking around?"

"No, it's not like that."

"C'mon, let's go." Saeed grabbed my wrist and tried to pull me out of the elevator, but I was so much taller than him that I wouldn't be moved. The doors began closing again and he kicked them back open, another unexpected response. "If you get caught it's going to be bad for everyone."

He was right. Even if I was fired the rest of the team would suffer from enhanced restrictions on things like phone time and access to television. But what Saeed didn't know—and how could he—was that I wouldn't be caught; there was no one to catch me.

"Christ man, let's go already." He struggled to find traction and as the elevator doors started closing, he discovered that this time they could not be stopped, and rather than allow him to be sandwiched between them and dragged for however long, I pulled him toward me and into the elevator car. The doors finally closed completely, the gasket between them sealing. Saeed was stuck with me.

"Great." He placed his fingers between the doors and attempted to pull them open, but they stayed firmly together, and soon we were moving. I hadn't punched in a floor number, but I knew where it was taking us.

"We could lose our jobs for this." A look of pure panic spread across Saeed's face, and he began to pull hard on his fingers, a nervous fidget I'd witnessed before. "Or worse, we could get arrested for trespassing. It's specifically in our contracts that we are not to visit any other areas of the site while unsupervised. How can you be so calm about this?"

I found it difficult to focus on what Saeed was saying. I was preoccupied by the quaking in my body, which had only grown in intensity as the elevator began to move.

"I'm going to get fired. That's it. I'm going to get fired, then I am going to have to move back home and suffer through my father's constant chiding." He sat on the floor and I sat down with him. "It wasn't easy to get this job, you know, not for me. Good pay and reasonable hours? Maybe you and your milky complexion can find that on any given day, but I had to wait and wait and scrape." The elevator dinged to let us know that we had advanced one floor. Two to go.

"You aren't going to lose your job." Then, before I could enforce better judgment, I relayed to him what Piotr had told me. By the time I finished the elevator had stopped moving.

"So how did you get the elevator to come?"

"I didn't. It was just there."

"So it was, what, 'calling' you? Are you on drugs?"

I hadn't told Saeed what happened to me the night before, about my father and I's shared vision. Given where our relationship currently stood, there was no way he'd even entertain the idea.

The doors opened onto the jobsite floor, and without thinking, as though something else was in control of my body, I stood and walked out of the elevator. Everything had reverted: the tear was once again running through the plastic covering the window, the guards were absent, and Ponshu rolled out from behind a sawhorse, the gears that powered its motion gnashing, teeth missing, and the spokes mangled from when I kicked it the night before. It approached me and I knelt down, extending my hand as though it were a house cat. It chunked toward me, surveilling with its red laser eye, and then pointed itself in the direction of The Spike as if to indicate my destination before roving off behind a corner and disappearing from view.

I brought my hands near to my face, expecting them to be shaking, but my body appeared to be totally still and in control of its facility. At a burst of cold wind from the open window I pulled the blanket tighter around myself and walked toward the plywood barrier; the tremor in my body amplified with each step. Behind me the elevator doors remained open, spilling antiseptic light into the darkened jobsite.

"What happened here? It wasn't like this earlier." Saeed stood before the torn window, and in seeing him peer out over the city I recalled dropping my phone, visualizing myself falling, head down like someone knifing into the water from a high platform. "This wasn't here earlier."

I was a person propelled, and I moved the plywood aside so that I could fit through.

"Don't." Saeed was beside me, cramped into the space between the barrier and the door, but I wasn't paying attention to him anymore. He was simply along for whatever ride upon which I was embarking. I placed my hands on the door and the energy that was spiraling around my body seemed to transfer into the metal through the tips of my fingers, a sensation that flooded me with warmth as if I were wading gradually into tropical water.

I felt Saeed's hand on my shoulder and through him a different energy found its way into my body. For a moment I was a conduit, the force against the door and the force on my shoulder mixing. As I heard Saeed say, "Let's go back," the door began to move until, finally, I could see The Spike rotating in its cradle, the core of The Pinnacle spinning.

I entered the chamber alone and the heavy door closed behind me. A cline of color filled the space, cycling through the spectrum. The Spike itself seemed to be spinning faster and as I stepped closer, I could feel warm air being thrown off the shaft. I was alone and I knew what it wanted. I wasted no time, extending my hands and allowing them to rest on the smooth shank, my entire upper half extended out over the banister, suspended over the many thousands of feet that extended deep into the earth.

Except—

I was again in New Haven, at my house. I could see the entire first floor as though I were sitting atop the fireplace mantle. Out the windows the sun was shining brightly, the flowers in the planter box in full bloom. When had we acquired a planter box? And the couches? They looked new, more contemporary than what we had purchased secondhand from one of Embry's friends. The potted umbrella tree in the corner had grown considerably, wooden stakes driven into the soil to help support its weight. Embry and my parents passed through the kitchen and sat down on the sofa. Embry's hair was newly dyed, fingers of purple running through the brown. My parents appeared older, though not by much, lines creasing their faces with greater depth, my father in orthopedic shoes secured by Velcro. They made conversation, my mother gesturing to the walls, which had been covered with a paisley wallpaper. A murmuration of small birds passed above the skylight, throwing pinprick shadows over everything, if only for a moment. All of this took place in total silence. They all looked toward the hallway leading to the spare bedroom, as though there was something unexpected coming from it. Embry excused herself and, after a moment in which my mother and father showed one another something on their phones, she returned cradling an infant that couldn't have been more than a few months old. My parents seemed unsurprised by its appearance. Instead, they seemed to fawn over it, to reach out and allow the child to grab their fingers, to pinch the fat of its thighs. A spiral of black hair swirled atop the baby's head, which it could barely hold up on its own, and as it tried and failed to force my father's finger into its mouth its face broke out in a look of pure joy, eyes going to slits, toothless gums exposed.

My mind folded itself over and over. The presence of my parents indicated that this was indeed my child, though it was also a child that didn't exist yet. Seeing the baby, or rather, witnessing the bliss on Embry's face as she kneaded its cheek, lit in me a flame of happiness for which I was totally unprepared. If I was capable of motion, if I could have stepped down from the mantle and entered this scene, I would have gone and held my child and kissed their forehead. I would have felt the warmth of that small, delicate body meld with the warmth of my own, our chests pressed together, our hearts beating their song to one another, call and response. I wanted to live in this moment for as long as possible, to take in the feeling and allow it passage into my bloodstream, to breathe it in again and again until my lungs were full only with the particles of air and time that existed in the space the five of us—Embry, myself, my parents, this child—occupied.

But I wasn't there, and there was nothing to capture. This was happening in some moment of time to which I had no access. Perhaps I would never have access. There were no traces of me in this moment, save my parents. Perhaps I was at work in The Pinnacle still, threading yards of ten-gauge cable. Or perhaps Embry had kept her promise, and after she learned of her pregnancy, had kicked me out of the house for the good of the child. Perhaps I was dead, having driven into a bridge abutment or calcifying my liver to the point of inoperability.

Everyone jerked their head toward the front door, and I could see the knob turning. A bright stream of light entered through the jamb, revealing the shadowy outline of an unknown person.

"Sir?"

The light which was now flooding my house increased, covered every surface and then narrowed to a tunnel, at the end of which was The Spike ceaselessly turning.

Don't go. Stay. Please.

"Sir, you need to come with us."

Hands fell upon my hands and the vision was fully gone. I was being pulled backward through the open chamber door and then turned around to face three men, two of which were armed like the guards who'd been standing outside The Spike during the day. The third was a slight, pudgy man in a Robison-Moon windbreaker. Saeed stood near the open elevator doors. He looked guilty and failed to make eye contact with me as I was guided past and into the awaiting elevator car. He joined us and stood with his back turned, facing the doors as the elevator moved at normal speed down to the barracks. It was still night, and when Saeed stepped off, I attempted to follow but one of the guards grabbed my bicep.

"Not here," the pudgy man said.

Saeed turned to me before the door closed again and mouthed, I'm sorry.

We began to move again, lower down The Pinnacle. The numbers on the floor indicator passed rapidly.

"Your friend was worried about you," the pudgy man said. "He's concerned. Frankly, it's not hard to see why. You could have gotten hurt."

I'd left my blanket up at the jobsite and my feet were freezing on the metal elevator floor. I knew enough that if I was being taken somewhere by these men that I should say as little as possible. The elevator came to a stop after five minutes at the tenth floor and the doors opened to a warren of concrete hallways and exposed plumbing. The pudgy man put a hand between my shoulder blades and guided me to a small, windowless room with a single metal chair. He instructed me to sit, which I did, and only then realized how exhausted my legs had become. He then gestured for the two guards to wait outside. He closed the door, and the sound was like that of jail bars slamming shut.

"So," the pudgy man squatted down on his calves, which made his thighs balloon beneath his jeans. "What's your ID number? Let's start with that."

I told him and he jotted it into a spiral notebook he removed from his pocket. I wasn't sure why they hadn't just fired me, why, at this moment, I wasn't being escorted out of the building. I considered for a moment that they might have me arrested, or worse. How far would they go to protect whatever secret I had stumbled upon? Perhaps the reason I wasn't present in the vision I'd had was because I was in jail.

"You know you weren't supposed to be up there, so I'm not going to ask you to be sorry." He stood and began to pace between the walls, a distance that was no larger than the length of a king size bed. "And you know what? I don't even care why you were up there. Your friend seems to think you were not in your right mind. Maybe that's true. After all, I'm not sure that it's worth risking your job over seeing something so mundane." He passed behind me and gripped the back of the chair. "No, what I care about is how you got up there to begin with. Do you smoke?" He took a crumpled packet of cigarettes from his back pocket and extended it to me.

I shook my head no.

"You're sure? Takes the edge off, you know."

He retrieved a cigarette and brought it to his lips, cupping his hand over it as he produced a lighter. "You don't mind, right?"

He didn't wait for an answer and pulled long, blowing the smoke out through his nose. "You have to understand, technically what you were doing is considered a breach of security, something we take very seriously. Again, I don't much care what you were doing up there, but I do need to know how you called the elevator."

I resisted the urge to tell him what Piotr had told me, about how the code had been the same since breaking ground on the foundation; how I now knew about the lapses in security. In the mind of this man The Pinnacle was some unassailable fortress filled with workers too exhausted to cause any real damage. After all, we were getting paid, why would we bite the hand that feeds?

"I didn't call it. It was just there."

"I thought you might say something like that." The man unzipped his windbreaker, taking it off and hanging it on a hook near the door. Adding to his bulk was a lead vest, the kind worn during dental X-rays, beneath which he had on a sweat-stained long-sleeve.

He adjusted the vest and returned the cigarette to his mouth, allowing it to hang loose off his lip. "But, you see, that isn't how it works. Somebody has to call for it. And only a few people know those codes. We keep them very secret."

I exhaled through my nose.

"Did I say something?" He bent over at eye level with me and exhaled into my face. "I'm going to ask you again: how did you call the elevator?"

"I really didn't. It was just there. I woke up and it was there." I was aware of how I looked and sounded. No shoes, frayed boxer shorts and an undershirt, raving about something I could barely explain. If I were down on the street, people would cross to avoid me.

The pudgy man spread a hand across his forehead, which was beginning to perspire, and rubbed his temples. "Where are you from? Were you born in this country?"

I told him that I was. I found it hard to believe that they didn't already know everything about me, given the degree to which we were surveilled.

"You ever live anywhere else? Saudi Arabia? China? Russia? Anywhere like that?"

I told him no. I wondered if, at any moment, he was going to strike me. I thought again of my vision, of the future in which I was not present. Perhaps I had been executed, here, in this room, to preserve some privileged information about which I had no tangible idea.

"Listen," the pudgy man gestured with his cigarette, the flaming point only a finger's width away from my eye. "I'm not stupid, and you're not stupid, though you've done a very stupid thing," with each utterance of the word "stupid" his spit flew against my face. "If you tell us how you got up there we'll only have you fired and not arrested, how's that?"

If I'd told him what really happened—or what I thought really happened—he would think that I was lying, that I was trying to subvert him in some way. The ramifications of that eddied in my mind. I didn't know what answer the pudgy man wanted, but I knew what answer I could not afford to give.

I responded with silence.

"I get it. You're trying your hardest. You work and you work and there's still not enough. So you snoop around. Maybe you'll find something you can leverage into more money. There's no room anymore for working class people. I understand." He placed a conciliatory hand on my shoulder and I flinched. I wasn't restrained in any way, but I still felt as though I couldn't move. "You're just trying to put bread on the table. Hey, so am I, right? Whatever you may think, we're not the bad guys. Everyone's just trying to secure what's theirs. I understand. Now, I'm going to ask again, how did you call the elevator?"

"I don't—"

It was as though an insect had bitten my skin, a fast, prickling sensation followed by the smell of burning hair. No, not hair, but flesh. I'd smelled it before. Working with live wires you're bound to get zapped a few times, and I'd lost fingernails and the hair on my knuckles from electrical burns before. Though this feeling lingered, I felt the left side of my face crawl with heat, my muscles involuntarily twitching. I reached up to bat away the cigarette that was burning in the skin beneath my eye, but the pudgy man kneed me in the groin before socking me hard in the gut and I found myself unable to combat him. Pain from two poles met in the center of my body and the idea that any of this was the product of some grand hallucination dissolved in an instant.

"I don't want to hear 'I don't know' again." The pudgy man pulled the cigarette back—which dragged along pieces of my stuck skin with it—and he pitched it into the corner, the flame having gone out on my face. "Next time, it's going in your eye."

My hands flung to the point of my newly acquired brand, and I could feel the lingering heat, the tenderness of the flesh now seared red and throbbing, blood rushing to the surface in a futile attempt to stay the damage.

I didn't blame Saeed for what was happening to me

at that moment. He had only done what any concerned friend would do. I was acting erratically as though possessed, and the chance that I could hurt myself—as demonstrated so many times in the last few days—was high. I only hoped that he wouldn't be forced to suffer a similar interrogation, but I knew that was unlikely. He was my friend, and I didn't want that for him.

"Maybe you just don't remember right now," the pudgy man said. "That's okay, we have time."

A shuddering ripple went through the walls and floor. I thought perhaps that the vibrations from before had returned, that I was again being summoned, but the pudgy man noticed it as well. Immediately after, a low, sinuous siren began to wail, accompanied by flashing white lights in the hallway outside the room. The pudgy man looked alarmed, and after opening the door to converse with one of the guards, turned to me and pointed his finger as though it were the bayonet at the tip of a rifle.

"Don't move. I'll be back." He grabbed his windbreaker and bolted out of the room, leaving me alone, glued to the chair as I waited for the pain to dissipate. Minutes passed and I could hear the hum of the elevator as it moved through the core of the building. Then, again. It seemed to be moving faster, over and over, ferrying people around The Pinnacle. The alarm noise had stopped, but the lights continued to flash. After hearing the cycle of the elevator move by the hallway for the fifth time I stood and eased toward the door, peeking through the gap in the jamb. The guards were gone, the hallway deserted. I opened the heavy door, which had not been locked, and stepped out into the strobe.

There were many different emergency scenarios for which we had been trained. Floods, blizzards, earthquakes—we were prepared. Though the prospect of anything like that happening was made all the more dangerous by the fact that, hundreds of floors up, taking the stairs down to street level may as well have been impossible. As such, we'd all have to cram into the elevator and pray that by the time whatever disaster had caught up to where we had been, that we were far enough away. I was far from being born at the time 9/11 happened, and most of the other laborers were in the U.S. only on work visas, so we perhaps didn't have the same appreciation others had for the very particular threats that can befall large buildings.

I had no idea what was going on in The Pinnacle at that moment. All I knew is that the pudgy man and the two accompanying guards had left to either investigate or flee from whatever was causing the alert. I saw in their absence a way to extract myself. After all, I was going to lose my job anyway, what further harm could be done by simply leaving? I approached the elevator—hobbled by my aching groin—and found that, while its doors were open, the car wasn't present, resulting in the terrifying image of the tall shaft rising up into a seemingly impenetrable darkness. I poked my head inside, bracing myself against the jamb, and saw in the blackness the cable begin to move. Somebody or something was coming, and I pulled my head back as the sound of screeching metal funneled down the shaft, followed by the moving car as it passed quickly by my floor on its way to the street, blowing cold air in my face. I waited, but the elevator car passed by me going up and down three times more, never once stopping, oblivious to the fact that I was there. This time, it wasn't coming for me.

I wandered the hallways. Around each corner another similar expanse of windowless concrete stretched out, a sort of motion given to it by the flashing lights. Along each wall were a series of small rooms, all exactly like the one I had just recently been inside: one aluminum chair, one ill-fitted heavy metal door with a cartoonishly large lock on the outside, a scratched plexiglass porthole. After every few steps I would stop and brush the concrete chips from the soles of my feet, my toes having lost sensation from the prolonged cold of the unfinished floor. The floor's layout seemed intentionally labyrinthine, every bend giving way to another unremarkable expanse of brutalist nothing. I began to feel as though I were making no progress at all, and I wasn't sure if I had been worming my way around for ten minutes or fifty. I imagined The Pinnacle suddenly collapsing or the hallways filling with water or a bomb going off in the underground garage. I couldn't tell if the noises I was hearing were the routine clanging of the exposed pipes that ran along the ceiling or the echo of footsteps somewhere behind me, their distance unknown.

I stopped and sat against the wall. Perhaps The Pinnacle was designed for inescapability. Whatever raged on the floors above and below me would find itself to my location soon. Immolation, starvation, laceration. I had no idea. Hopelessness sat on my chest, and I physically gripped around my breastbone as though I could grab hold of it. I stood and began to move again, navigating the hallways via a combination of ragged running and slow, deflated walking.

I thought of Embry in the most recent vision, of the baby, our baby. We'd made love before I left, and the wheel could already be turning to make The Spike's vision into reality. I wanted desperately to meet that vision, to emerge on the other side of whatever timeline I was traversing. I wanted to be the one coming through that door.

I turned another corner and then, like someone's outstretched hand in my face, there was a wall. I leaned against it and found my breath sharp and ragged, my throat coated with mucus. I had been running, passing by the endless doors as though on a treadmill. There was one final door, and looking through the window I expected a similar reproduction of what I had seen before, but instead there was a narrow concrete staircase no wider than the width of my shoulders. A stairway made more sense this far down The Pinnacle, though as I pushed through the door the lights that dotted the wall flickered off, leaving only the intermittent strobe of the alarm light to guide me. I had no idea where these stairs would deposit me, and feeling my way along the walls in the periodic darkness I felt as though I was descending deep into the earth, and that when I emerged, I would be surrounded by quartz crystal thick as my arm or cascades of molten rock turning the sand below to a smooth sheet of glass.

Running down the steps, the broadside of my shoulder soon collided with smooth, cold metal: a door. I put the whole weight of my body into the crash bar and as it creaked open the flashing lights of the alarm were replaced by the flashing lights of countless fire trucks, their alternating blue and red splashed and reflected against the polished side of The Pinnacle's exterior.

Bands of orange and purple draped across the sky, smothering the stars with pre-dawn. Through the chain-link fence that surrounded the building's footprint a man was pushing up the rolling metal gate that protected the windows of a shoe store. Surrounding me on both sides were pallets of concrete mix, the faint smell of ammonia and early morning cold. A single pigeon perched on the telescoping ladder of one of the fire trucks took flight and landed in front of me, expecting food. I was back on Earth. I turned around and found that the door I'd come through was exit only, the space where a handle would normally be polished smooth. I was sealed out.

Careful to avoid stray nails and screws littered over the packed dirt foundation I made my way toward a din of conversation taking place by the main elevators. There were nearly a hundred people huddled outside the elevator doors, some of which were being pushed back from The Pinnacle by firefighters passing extinguishers to one another and depositing them in the open elevator car. Half of the people were dressed like me, clad in some loose assemblage of pajamas, the other half were men I had never seen before in gray jumpsuits, many of whom held hard hats in their hands. Everyone was looking up. I joined them.

There were no clouds just yet, and in the faint sun I could just see to the top of The Pinnacle, its exposed rebar like spikes puncturing the sky. What I thought was the sunrise reflecting off the building's many glass panels turned out to be an intense fire that had blown out several of the windows. The distance made it so that the blaze itself was silent, like looking at television footage taken from a helicopter high over the ground. I attempted to count the floors down from the top. In my estimation the fire was burning through the 324th floor, the same floor we'd been working on for the past several days.

There was then a hand on my shoulder.

"I grabbed this for you."

Saeed handed me my duffle bag. He still had on the same clothes he was wearing when I was taken away by the pudgy man.

"I figured, you know, if I saw you again, I'd give it to you."

"Thanks." It was a kindness I had not expected.

"I'm sorry for calling the company on you, really. I just thought, I don't know, that there was something wrong."

I could tell he was staring at my face, or rather staring around the burn coiled beneath my eye, avoiding it. He began to ask what happened but stopped himself and looked back up at the fire.

"It's okay. Thank you for this." I reached out and put a hand on his shoulder, a gesture he was clearly unprepared for, and gave an affirming squeeze, which acted as a sort of conversational reset. "Do you know what's going on?"

"No more than you. The alarms went off and they shuffled us into the elevator and here we are. Noor says we're supposed to meet up by the server trailer in five minutes."

"Does she know?"

"About you? I don't think so. She was pretty harried getting us all out."

"Huh." We watched the far-away fire burn until Saeed gestured that it was time to meet up with the team, all of whom were rubbing their arms in an effort to stay warm in the early morning. A large crowd had gathered at the fence, taking grainy video on their cell phones.

Noor, too, was in pajamas, though hers consisted of a full two-piece set in purple silk. Her initials were monogrammed over the breast pocket, within which was a bulky walkie-talkie. She took roll, and while I was apprehensive to affirm that I was present, nothing came of it. Perhaps she hadn't known that I'd been questioned, that I trespassed. When she finished, I realized that she had skipped Piotr's name entirely. She then told us that we were to go home, and we would have the next week off while the site was made safe, and that we would be paid for the time. She spoke calmly, as though there wasn't a fire raging behind us that threatened the tallest building in the history of the planet.

"You will receive all further updates via your company email," she yelled over an oncoming emergency siren. With that, she stepped off the apple box she had been standing on and walked in the direction of one of the managerial trailers, speaking into the walkie-talkie.

Saeed asked if he could give me a ride home—out of what I assumed was a lingering guilt—but I told him that it was fine, and we parted ways for what I imagined was the last time. I fished a pair of flip-flops from my bag, donned a jacket, and as I was crossing the threshold that separated The Pinnacle from the rest of the city, I looked back to make sure that the pudgy man wasn't following me, that I could actually escape. I walked to Grand Central and called Embry collect from a disgusting payphone—perhaps the last one still operating in Manhattan—asking her to buy me a train ticket back to New Haven. I told her that there had been a fire, and that I'd had no time to get my wallet in the evacuation. She purchased a ticket on her phone and then gave me the confirmation number.

"But you're okay?" she asked.

"Yeah. I want to come home."

"Okay, yeah, please."

I had two hours to wait until I could leave the city, which gave me just enough time to fall asleep while reading a week-old *Sunday Times* someone had left on top of a garbage can.

I was sitting on the couch when I learned I'd been fired.

Embry had brought in the mail, within which was a slim Robison-Moon branded envelope addressed to me. It gave no specific reason for my termination, only stating that I had forfeited my right to any severance pay and was barred from applying to any future positions at the organization. The letter concluded with a notice that, in accepting a position at Robison-Moon, I had given consent to a legally binding non-disclosure agreement which, if violated, would result in immediate and severe punitive action. This was most likely a boilerplate form, but I couldn't help but read the last paragraph as a sort of veiled threat aimed directly at me. Though if my being fired was the only consequence of what happened at The Pinnacle then I suppose I should have been grateful.

I texted Saeed from my new phone and told him the news. He told me he wasn't surprised. The fire, which had been extinguished after fifteen grueling hours, had slowed the company's work on the project significantly. Later we would learn that the ceiling mounted sprinklers had never been hooked up to water and were totally defunct. Had there been a team working at the time they would have likely all been killed.

Saeed added that Robison-Moon was now laying off people by the dozens. I knew that I wasn't let go as a result of some cost saving measure, but I didn't tell Saeed this. I asked him if they figured out what started the fire and he responded that he didn't know. Then, after I didn't respond, he texted:

You didn't...Did you?

I told him no but couldn't say if it assuaged his doubt.

The fire got very little coverage in the press. Perhaps Robison-Moon had the news covered up. Not even the myriad cell phone camera footage made it anywhere noteworthy. It all seemed to simply disappear.

I set my phone on the end table and turned on the television. Embry soon joined me on the couch, and we watched a competition baking show. She threw a piece of popcorn toward me and I caught it in my mouth with ease. I'd been home for a week. I'd also been sober for a week, which was the longest continuous stretch of me living in New Haven and not finding myself at the bottom of a bottle. On television the contestants were making self-portraits out of cake. She was upset with me, clearly. I had lost my job, and with it the income upon which we depended. I couldn't shake the feeling that our relationship was perched at a cliff's edge, steadied only by my promise that I would somehow repair myself. The first night after I got back from The Pinnacle I had been made to sleep on the couch, after which Embry and I had a long discussion about "the future." I was to find a job in New Haven. I was to attend meetings. I was to show her the places where I had stashed alcohol around the house. How she knew about these I wasn't sure. Though even more surprising is that I was relieved to finally have been constrained. Upon hearing that I could no longer work in the city or spend nights in bars across town it was as though a great weight had dissolved from around my body. I hadn't told her about my last vision yet. If it were indeed a foretelling, I would let it play out on its own.

My fledgling sobriety made me think often about Piotr. I had no idea what happened to him after the elevator doors closed. I assume he was found and then fired, forced out of The Pinnacle for the first time in many years where his vices would again discover and devour him. When I go to the city, which isn't often, I take careful note of all the homeless men I come across, hoping not to see Piotr among them, if he's even still alive.

He remains one of several mysteries that surround The Pinnacle. It is still not publicly known what happened to the team we were replacing. The possibility exists that they banded together and walked off the jobsite in protest, though about what no one is sure. That's the rumor, anyway, Saeed has told me. At night, lying in bed with nothing but my thoughts and the quiet hum of Embry's soft snoring, the images transmitted to me by The Spike return with vivid detail. Perhaps the previous team experienced similar visions. Perhaps they became lost within them somehow, vanishing into some imagined future.

Embry paused the show so that she could open the back door for the dog, and while waiting for her to return I flipped through social media on my phone. There, below a photo of my cousin's newborn daughter, was a large poster-like graphic, the words "sponsored content" captioned in red beneath it.

Help build history! Robison-Moon is looking for qualified construction professionals for upcoming projects near you!

This was accompanied by a photo of workers standing triumphantly on a completed floor, hands on their hips like a squadron of superheroes.

I hit the menu icon above the post and selected "not interested," after which it disappeared, replaced seamlessly by an ad for a submarine sandwich.

ACKNOWLEDGMENTS

Unlimited gratitude goes out to Joshua James Amberson, Gabriel Urza, Michael Heald, Sean Cummings, and Tim Day, all of whom read early versions of this book. Your patience and kindness are immeasurable.

Thank you to my parents, whose support is unconditional.

And, of course, thank you to Kiku and Loren, who endlessly inspire.

ABOUT

BENJAMIN KESSLER is the author of the story collection *Of This World (Game Over Books, 2023)*. His writing has appeared in *DIAGRAM*, *Bellevue Literary Review*, and *Pithead Chapel*, among others. He occasionally teaches, frequently thrifts, and lives happily with his family in Portland, Oregon.

FOREST WOLF KELL is a multidisciplinary artist and designer from Portland, Oregon. Primarily his works are collections of objects, images, and icons arranged in ways meant to provoke thought.

www.ingramcontent.com/pod-product-compliance
Lightning Source LLC
Chambersburg PA
CBHW060511300726

48975CB00008B/2736